Simone's Secret

Also available in the Angel Light™ series:
Angela's Answer (Book One)

BOOK TWO

AngelLight

Simone's Secret

—◦ PAT MATUSZAK ◦—

An Imprint of AMG Publishers.

First printing—November 2009

Cover designed by Left Coast Design, Portland, Oregon

Interior design and typesetting by Reider Publishing Services, West Hollywood, California

Edited and proofread by Rich Cairnes, Dan Penwell, and Rick Steele

Printed in the United States of America
14 13 12 11 10 09 –V– 7 6 5 4 3 2 1

Dedication

This book is dedicated to my wonderful family who inspired it, and especially to my daughter, Christi, and granddaughter, Hannah, who helped me write it.

Note to readers:

This is the second book in the Angel Light series of fictional stories. It is not meant to portray real people, places, or events. It is not written to be a theological guide, though the author hopes it will inspire readers to be guided by the One who is life's true light.

Psalm 91: 9–11

For more information on Simone, Angela, and their friends, and to find clues about what will happen next, go online to:

www.AngelClues.com

Point Zero in Paris

Contents

♪

Acknowledgments

WITHOUT THE prayer and encouragement of family and friends, and the grace and inspiration of the One who answers prayer, I could not have written this book.

Many thanks to those at AMG who continue to generously guide my efforts, especially Dan Penwell who acquired it, Rick Steele who sustained it, Rich Cairnes who honed it, and the rest of the team who spent many hours skillfully supporting their work to produce and deliver the copy you hold in your hands.

About St. Patrick

When we hear the name Saint Patrick, we might think of leprechauns and wearing green on St. Patrick's Day, but just as there was a real man named St. Nicholas whose life started the legend of Santa Claus, there was a real man named St. Patrick whose life started a legend.

Patrick was a missionary to Ireland around AD 400 who is said to have converted thousands of Picts and Irish people to Christianity. He lived as an equal with the people to whom he preached the gospel message and led them to Christ by his own example as a believer among them.

Patrick was a real missionary with a serious purpose to his life and dedication to serve God and people. The prayers he prayed were serious prayers. The stories of him driving snakes out of Ireland and the tradition of wearing green shamrocks were added to his legend for fun, long after his death, the same way reindeer and elves were added to the story of St. Nicholas.

The Prayer of Saint Patrick

Protect me, Christ, till thy returning.

Christ be with me, Christ within me,

Christ behind me, Christ before me,
 Christ beside me, Christ to win me,

Christ to comfort and restore me,
Christ beneath me, Christ above me,

Christ in quiet, Christ in danger,
Christ in hearts of all that love me,

Christ in mouth of friend and stranger.
I bind unto myself the name,
The strong name of the Trinity;

By invocation of the same.
 The Three in One, and One in Three,

Of whom all nature hath creation,
 Eternal Father, Spirit, Word:

Praise to the Lord of my salvation,
salvation is of Christ the Lord.

A Secret Place and a Secret Plan

IMONE'S RED VW Beetle sputtered up to the locked gate at the entrance to the U-Stor-Em lot. Considering its age, the Bug wasn't in bad shape, just a little squeaky and the seats a little lumpy. It had been her mom's cool car in college, but by the time she handed it down to Simone, it was a beater. The black convertible top still worked, but it creaked in protest when Simone put it down to get a breeze. In winter, the heater was too feeble to keep her feet warm on really cold days. It was getting too cold to be out in the Bug after the sun went down. However, she'd soon be done with hiding out after dark.

Matt, the storage lot attendant, put on a surly expression whenever he saw a car pull up to the keypad lock. He was actually a nice-looking guy if you saw him around town, when he wasn't working for his uncle at the lot. He didn't like to be bothered by customers with questions after dark, though, so he did what he could to discourage conversation. But when he saw that it was Simone at the gate, he smiled and waved.

A lot of guys had that reaction to her when they first saw her—friends described her as "cute," a tiny girl with curly, dark hair and long eyelashes and dark brown eyes. When she just thought about smiling, and sometimes even if she were frowning intensely, dimples formed in her cheeks. Her looks were deceptive, however, because Simone was a driven woman.

2

♪

She was serious about life in general and passionate about only one thing—her music. It made her burning mad when guys, especially if they were musicians, didn't take her seriously just because of outward appearances. She had to face that prejudice every time she got her saxophone out to play. But she overcame it in the first few minutes of a performance. Maybe she even tried *too* hard at times. When she won the competition for section leader over the sax players in the high school band, they all started calling her "Master" to try to get her to lighten up.

"Hi, Matt," Simone called as she waved back to the attendant, trying to keep her expression neutral. She didn't want to encourage conversation, but she also didn't want to offend the gatekeeper to her secret venue.

She locked her car door as she drove into the lot. The storage garages were deserted at this time of night. Good. But the rows of identical doorways cast long shadows in the gloom and the vents in the doors looked like eyes that followed her car as she drove to the end of the row. The area was well lit, but the fluorescent bulbs flickered just enough to make it seem like something had moved at the corner of her vision.

Silly, silly girl, Simone told herself. *This is a nice suburban town. There's nothing to worry about, especially locked in a fenced area with a security guard.* Maybe Matt would walk down the row to see she got safely into her unit, as he sometimes did. He would stand at the entrance gate and wait for her to give a wave to let him know she didn't have any trouble opening the door or anything. She looked over her shoulder, but she didn't see his silhouette behind her.

She was almost to her unit: number 23 at the end of row 1. *Wait . . . what was that? Another optical illusion from the lights, probably.* She looked again. *Oh, no!* A rapid blink did not change what she had seen.

Something really had moved. A dark figure leaned out of the shadow and stepped into the light. Simone hit the brakes, sliding in the gravel beneath its wheels before coming to a stop. Her heart raced as if it were going to escape her chest. She gasped, rather than screamed, but the figure now walking toward her car had heard it.

"You okay, Simone?" a guy's voice asked as the figure pulled a wool cap off his head and looked into the car window.

3
♪

Whew! It was just Adam. He had been lounging against the door of the last unit and she hadn't seen him until he stepped out of the shadow.

"You scared me," she said, out of breath. With everything else she had experienced lately, all this sneaking around was too much drama. She hoped it would be worth it in the end.

"After all we've been through the past couple of weeks, I can see why a dark alley would make you jumpy," the tall boy said, smiling and giving her shoulder a pat as she got out of the car. "I've been a little nervous, too, out here in the dark by myself. I was hoping you'd be here before me with the key."

They really had gone through a weird adventure together. Their friends Teri and Marti had been kidnapped by a stranger, who turned out to be stranger than anyone had guessed—a creature with supernatural powers. They had pieced it all together at lunch the day after the big rescue.

Simone had seen the actual kidnapping. And it was like something out of a sci-fi movie, complete with Teri disappearing through a doorway where there had been only a solid brick wall, the creature performing some kind of scary ritual, and a rescue by someone who looked every bit like a real angel right out of a Bible illustration.

Simone and Adam had watched the whole thing, as if on a movie screen, through the mysterious door in the wall, but they could not pass through it to help. When they saw that their friends had been rescued, they scrambled for their cell phones and started calling them. All they got was voice mail, of course. They didn't get the full story until they met everyone at their usual lunch table the next day.

Teri and Marti weren't sure about all the details because they had been hypnotized or something by the creature's ritual. Their friends Angela and Kyle had been part of the rescue, but they had few answers. No one knew everything about what had happened. It seemed as if solving one mystery just opened a whole *new* set of questions.

"Can I help you with that?" Adam asked, interrupting Simone's thoughts as she unloaded the trunk of her car. She passed him the heavy tenor sax case that contained her Selmer Mark VI, another vintage hand-me-down from her mom. He shouldered the bulky instrument case as if it weighed nothing, and carried it alongside his even larger baritone sax case.

"Thanks, Adam. Sorry to keep you waiting."

"Hey, it's worth the wait. Better than last year. Football equipment is almost as heavy, but not as much fun."

Adam was probably the most serious musician in the sax section besides Simone. He was a big, strong guy and he looked the part of a high school athlete, but he had found it an easy decision to give up a sure spot on the football team to play bari sax in the band.

Simone jiggled the key into the rusty lock on the side door of the unit. When it finally opened, her hand

5
♪

searched the wall inside. She found the switch and the warm yellow light blinked on. Simone smiled to see her drum kit all set up just as she had left it last time. It was like an old friend waiting for her. She couldn't wait to play some music. To do something so normal would be comforting. Life was good.

"Ah, let there be heat," Adam said as he flipped on a small space heater.

Simone had used the storage unit for a practice room when she first got the kit—another hand-me-down, this one from a friend of her mom. She didn't want anyone to know she was learning a new instrument until she got good at it.

She wasn't going to be the one doing the drumming today. They heard a car pull up outside. Doors opening and closing meant the rest of her band had arrived. She held the small side door open to let them in, keeping the big garage door shut to hold in the little bit of warmth the space heater churned out. Adam leaned over her shoulder and looked outside. "There they are, and they've brought the groupies, I see."

Simone frowned. She wanted to rehearse, not party. There was nothing to party about until after their plan came together, but Conan, Greg, and Moby didn't go anywhere without their girlfriends, and the girls didn't go anywhere without a couple of their friends, fearing they'd be bored. Simone could only hope they'd actually get bored and go for a snack run so the guys wouldn't be distracted. She had to admit the girls were respectful of their rehearsal time, but the group interacted differently without an audience. There would be plenty of time for audiences next week when they were going on tour. It had always been her dream to tour with a band, and now she was getting the chance to spend next week's fall break from school doing just that—and with her very own band. She just wished it wasn't for a competition. Touring and playing together in front of an audience would be enough pressure. Having judges from a band competition in the audience would make it much more stressful.

2

A Few Answers

THE HEAVY front door of the old farmhouse swung open. Angela leaned out and an icy breeze caught her long, dark hair and threw it to one side. She reached for her best friend and pulled the tiny girl into the warm foyer as another wind gust threatened to slam the door. She held it open for a second longer and looked around the corner.

"Where's Simone?"

Marti shrugged, pulled off her wool scarf, and fluffed out her spiky blond hair. "My dad dropped me off. Simone couldn't give me a ride because she had to practice. She said she might drop by later, but wasn't sure."

Angela led the way to the big country kitchen. "Hmmm. Adam called earlier and said the same thing. There must be something coming up with the marching

band. But Teri and Michelle made it here, so only half the
sophomores in the saxophone section are practicing late.
Kyle, Billy Joe, and Chuck are here, too. They're in the
kitchen with my family. We have bed-and-breakfast guests
at the farm this week, so we can't use the library for our
meeting. But there's plenty of room in the breakfast
nook."

Marti sighed, comforted by the thought of seeing all
her friends and talking about anything besides her parents' marriage problems. She'd had a long week. Her
mom and dad were back together after almost divorcing,
but the counseling sessions they'd agreed to go to felt like
hard work.

The big country kitchen was the perfect setting for
Marti to shed her stress along with her jacket. The long,
wooden breakfast table with its sturdy benches and chairs
stretched out far enough to hold her friends along with
Angela's parents, two aunts, and little brother, Bren. The
lively group passed around huge bowls of popcorn, plates
of cookies, and pitchers of apple cider.

"Hi, Marti," a tall, dark, and handsome guy in a cowboy shirt called out as she turned the corner into the
kitchen. Billy Joe Countryman flashed her one of his mil-
lion-dollar smiles and held out a chair for her. She used
to think he was impossible to like, but after all they'd been
through together he now seemed impossible *not* to like.
Marti had seen the positive side to his overbearing per-
sonality when he'd boldly faced down a demonic kidnapper to rescue her and their friends. Beneath his brash

9

exterior, there hid a quiet strength—a strength she wanted to learn more about.

She sat down next to Billy Joe and his younger brother. Chuck was engrossed in conversation with her friend Teri, who waved to Marti, then flipped her long, blond hair behind her shoulder before her blue eyes locked back on Chuck's. The two didn't even try to deny they had become a couple after they rode off into the sunset together on Chuck's horse following the big rescue. To describe the scene sounded like the ending to a corny Western, but no one tried to laugh it off. Somehow, seeing it in person had been anything but corny.

There was another scene everyone remembered from that day, but no one knew what to say about it exactly. The problem was that they had no real-life experience talking about meeting an angel.

"What do you say about something like that?" Michelle had asked, shaking her head and her silky, black ponytail when they'd all met at lunch the next day. Michelle usually had something to say about everything, something pithy (and often sarcastic), so it was strange for her to admit to being shocked into speechlessness. And she hadn't even seen the angel in person. She and Adam and Simone had watched the supernatural rescue helplessly through a mysterious doorway that appeared in the band room wall. "It was beyond sci-fi . . ."

"It was real," said Angela's mom, pausing near them as she laid a stack of Bibles in the middle of the table and

10
♪

got everyone's attention. "Here are some reference books. Since we've learned Emerald Circle Valley is a point of interest for heavenly and not-so-heavenly beings, I think we'd better get some perspective on all this from Heaven's sourcebook."

"Yeah, I guess there are some things we don't need to be open-minded about now that we've seen the stairway to Heaven with our own eyes," Teri said, shaking her head in embarrassment. They all remembered how she'd scolded them for rejecting Marti's faith in the crystals Clé gave her.

"Well, who would ever suspect Clé was a fallen angel and not just a guy trying to give presents to a pretty girl?" Chuck said, trying to make her feel better.

"How can regular people know anything about angels?" asked Michelle.

"That's the reason we have to meet and sort things out—if we're going to be involved in a war between angels, we don't want to become pawns. We need to find out how to tell heavenly angels from fallen angels," said Kyle. "If a fallen angel can look like an ordinary kid, like Clé did, we have to figure out how to identify them before they have a chance to kidnap anyone else."

Angela's aunt Candace felt sure the golden creature who had come to their rescue at the cottage was a good angel. "He had all the right biblical answers. But more than that, he 'felt right.' There was a kind of peace that flowed all around him," Aunt Candace said.

"And he took charge of that creature—Clay or Clé— whatever his name really was," Kyle agreed.

11
♪

"I think the angel was calling him Clé," said Angela. "That means *key* in French and he had a key to the doors that opened The Lines, so that makes the most sense."

Marti nodded. "We just thought of a more common name when we heard it the first time. But whatever Clé was, he wasn't common. He was stranger than any stranger we've ever met."

"And he was the opposite in every way of the angel who rescued us," said Teri. "I'm sure that creature was an angel. I mean, who walks up through the sky on stairs made of light besides angels?"

"Aliens?" Michelle laughed, recovering her sense of humor.

"Yeah, I don't think so," Angela said. "He seemed like someone who belongs here, even if he did come from Heaven. Like he just loved it here and loved us. Like a dad would." She nodded to her own dad sitting in the big, old creaky rocking chair at the end of the table. Smile lines crinkled his tanned, leathery face as he spoke.

"That all sounds good as a theory, but let's agree we make our first rule in this discussion to find the Bible verse to support what we believe. And let's pray before we talk more." He stood, took off his red Ohio State baseball cap, and then bowed his head. They all followed his lead. "Lord God of all wisdom, we come asking for understanding and your guidance. We know you are the source of all truth and we want to follow your path. Protect us from deception and sin as we seek to be your servants. In Jesus' name we pray. Amen."

"Dad, do you think the demon was able to capture us because of sin?" Angela's little ten-year-old brother, Bren, piped up before their dad had a chance to sit down.

"That's a good question," Mr. Clarkson answered patiently, picking up a Bible before sliding into his chair. "Let's talk about sin for a minute. Sin is breaking God's commandments. Let's look at Mark 12:29-30, the verses where Jesus tells us what the most important commandment is. Will you read it aloud, Bren?"

Bren shuffled through his Bible to find the verses, then stood and pushed a shock of blond hair away from his startling blue eyes. "It says, 'Jesus answered, "The most important one says: 'People of Israel, you have only one Lord and God. You must love him with all your heart, soul, mind, and strength.' " ' "

His dad nodded and winked at him, pleased with Bren's reading, and then said, "That's right. So if we put anything we want ahead of God and what he wants for us, we are breaking that commandment."

"Obeying commandments sounds more like something from the Old Testament," Angela said, frowning. "How can God command us to love him? Isn't love a feeling?"

Dad smiled. "Maybe romantic-movie love is a feeling. Real-life, deep-down love is a choice. I choose to show you love when I fulfill my role as a father. We choose to show our love to God when we fulfill our roles as his children and disciples by obeying his commandments. All his rules were given to place us under his protection.

13

♪

When we want our own way and decide to break them, we leave his protection. It's like walking out from under an umbrella into the rain. And there are things at stake more dangerous than getting wet. In 1 Peter 5:8 the Bible says the Enemy walks about the earth like a lion seeking whom he may devour."

"So if we have something in our hearts that we put ahead of what we know God would want, it's a sin?" asked Bren.

"Yes. And whether you have done that is a question you have to ask yourself and answer for yourself," Mr. Clarkson said. "Other people can't see into your heart, but you and God can. You have to judge yourself about that. It's important to recognize what tempts you, because the enemies of God and of our souls can take advantage of those things."

"Like that demon at the cottage." Bren felt a shiver go up his spine as he remembered.

"Do we really know Clé was a demon?" asked Marti.

"What else could he have been? The angel said he was the same kind of being, but was led by a liar. If he's a lying angel, that's a demon," said Billy Joe.

"Okay, remember our rule: Find the Bible verse to prove the truth," Kyle added, pushing his oversize glasses back up on his nose.

Billy Joe looked irritated for a second, but then he quickly began flipping through a Bible to prove he knew what he was talking about. Kyle was only a sophomore and looked even younger next to Billy Joe, who was a senior this year and had almost a foot height advantage. But the younger boy's determination to keep the group on the right track would not be denied. He meant to look out for his friends from now on, so he wasn't going to keep the scriptural truth he'd learned in church all his life to himself anymore. Angela smiled at her best guy friend and gave him a nod.

"That's right, Kyle," Mr. Clarkson agreed. "I can give you one for that off the top of my head, but I'm not sure where to find it. Can someone look this up in the concordance? 'The devil is a liar and the father of lies.'"

"That's the book of John, chapter 8, at verse 44. It's Jesus' own words," said a deep voice from the back corner of the room. They all turned to look and there was Thomas Chester, Angela's uncle, standing by the door, putting a leather briefcase on the floor. Aunt Candace stood up and practically ran to greet him, delighted to see her husband home from a late rehearsal with the Cleveland Symphony. The big man picked up his tiny, red-haired spouse as easily as he might have lifted a child, and laughed in a resounding baritone. "Honey, you look great today! I'll have to hide you from my boss for a while so he won't think I gave him a false excuse to come home from the tour early."

"You didn't tell him she saw you playing with the symphony through the angel window at the hospital, did you?" asked Angela. While Thomas was performing at the old opera house in Paris, Aunt Candace had seen him

15
♪

through a strange window that appeared in her hospital room. When she tried to go to him through it, she found herself transported through a secret system, which the group called The Angel Lines. From what they'd learned from the actual angel who appeared to help in their rescue, The Lines were some form of supernatural transportation used by believers who lived there long before their town was a town. The angel had also hinted that he had helped slaves use The Lines to escape via the Underground Railroad in times past.

"I did not tell my boss about what Candace saw," Thomas answered Angela, adding mysteriously, "nor did I tell him what I'd seen."

Candace turned to the group and said, "We have something to tell you about The Lines. We aren't sure what to conclude about this, but Thomas was also able to see me from Paris."

The room became still, as if everyone were holding his or her breath. What did this mean? If Candace had really seen Thomas, and it hadn't been a false vision caused by Clé to trick her, did that mean there was another of The Angel Lines that extended all the way to France?

The ones they had discovered in town seemed to lead only to each other and to an abandoned cottage Clé had used as his hideout. What if they also connected to other places?

3

Recurring Dream

SIMONE FELT exhausted after their rehearsal in the storage room and a cold ride home in her almost-unheated car. She'd fallen asleep as soon as her toes found a cozy corner of her bedspread to wrap up in. The sound of thunder woke her from a very sound sleep sometime later. She didn't know what time it was, but it was pitch black outside.

Except for one softly glowing street lamp. It was raining lightly, but little flashes of light and rumbles of thunder suggested it had not yet moved away. Wait a minute! There weren't any street lamps outside her house! Certainly not any gas lamps like the one she was looking at outside her second-story room. Simone sat up and walked slowly to the window. This wasn't her bedroom window, either. She touched the old leaded glass, warped a bit with little air bubbles scattered throughout. The window had small rectangular panes welded together into a nine-foot-tall frame with an old-fashioned latch and no screen. The walls around it were made of weathered blocks of stone, like those in a castle. This wasn't her room. Then it all came back to her. She was going to see the angel again.

Simone usually hated recurring dreams, like the one where she was falling or the one where she was at school and couldn't remember which classroom to go to next. But this dream was different. This one fascinated her. She could see the cobblestone street below reflecting moonlight and lamplight in its shiny coating of rain. Simone opened the window and felt a wave of crisp night air wash into the room.

Then Simone heard footsteps approaching from both directions on the street. In a few seconds, she saw the tops of two black umbrellas coming out of the shadows from opposite directions. On the right, she heard a sharp tap with each step and saw a woman's black high-heeled shoes as they moved out alternately from under the protective arch of the umbrella. On the left, there came the scuffing noise of a pair of men's brown oxfords stepping briskly across the cobblestones. Neither person paused, but as the two umbrellas passed each other they both made a little dip as if their owners had nodded a greeting to each other. Then the umbrellas continued on their separate ways and disappeared back into the darkness. The street below was empty now. It looked lonely, glowing in the mist. No more thunder sounded and the rain came to a stop.

Simone turned around and there was the first door. She then remembered that this dream had four doors for her to go through before she met the angel. The first door seemed to be just an ordinary wooden door. At first, she saw what she thought was the usual grain of the wood. But then there was a muffled sound, like a moan, that seemed to be coming from the other side of the door. She stayed where she was. With the heavy door closed, whatever was making the noise was shut outside. That seemed like a good thing.

It's funny how you forget the details of some dreams and find yourself repeating the same actions, even though you know better, Simone thought. *I could tell myself to wake up right now and I'd forget all about this.* It was true. But she waited to remember what to do next, because she wanted to see the angel again.

19

Just as she was getting ready to open the door, she remembered why she was waiting. The door was supposed to open on its own. The grain in the wood was morphing into a face. It was a sad face, with hollow eyes and a down-turned mouth, the kind of face you might imagine while looking at the patterns in the bark of a tree. The mouth was partially opened, and it moved in time with the moaning sound.

Simone would have been very frightened to see such a thing in the waking world, but here it didn't feel any more out of place than the gas lamp or the old glass window. It just struck her as sad. Then she realized why. The door face was not only moaning—it was talking! The words were forming so slowly it had taken her some time to recognize them.

"It's all right. It's all right. It's just me," the door face said. Brown tears like varnish streaks were forming at the corners of its eyes and running down the sides of the door. "Go ahead. It's okay," the face said and the door began to open by itself.

The outer side of the door was painted white, with no wood grain to see, so once the door opened up, the face disappeared. Just beyond the door was a beautiful spiral staircase made of marble steps going down, with intricate brass railings. The walls were white and well-lit by candle wall sconces and a grand chandelier overhead.

Simone remembered she always felt at home on the staircase, even though she had never lived in such a palace in her waking life. Maybe it was the golden glow that lit the room. It felt like a fresh summer morning. Walking down the white steps, she felt as if she were going to breakfast, because there was the lovely scent of fresh bread baking in the oven. When she reached the bottom of the stairs she saw the second door.

To get to it she had to cross an entrance foyer with a gray flagstone floor that was partially covered with a green woven carpet. Next to the door a vase of enormous pink tulips on a white marble-topped table caught her eye. Under the table lay a sleepy brown hound dog that yawned and wagged its tail in a friendly way when it saw her, but didn't bother to get up. The door was painted dark red and looked larger than a normal entrance door. Simone tried to open it, but although the brass doorknob turned easily enough, a deadbolt lock held it shut. She struggled to slide the lock to one side and when it finally gave way, she muscled the huge door open by shoving her shoulder against it.

Stepping outside Simone found herself in a beautiful walled courtyard that looked like part of a castle. Well-tended trees and flowers bloomed beside a stone path that led to a circular walk in the center of the courtyard. There were three women in black-and-white nuns' habits walking around the circular path, and Simone could hear them repeating the same words over and over as they moved with their heads bowed in prayer: "Christ behind me, Christ before me, Christ in hearts of all that love me."

Simone followed the women around the circle and out the other side. The path continued to the third door of her familiar dream. This door stood open and led into a grand cathedral, its far wall nearly filled by a huge, shining rose window made of stained glass in every color of the rainbow. As each of the nuns walked through the door, they disappeared into the dark interior, as if becoming part of the shadows on either side of the window, the great room's main source of light.

Dozens of little, white candle jars glowed on long tables beside the door. As Simone entered, she picked up one of the candles and carried it so she could more clearly see the aisle before her. She held the small light

21

carefully as she walked toward the altar under the rose window. When she reached it, she stood looking up at the enchanting glass design and wondering what to do next.

Then she heard the music. A soft, pure melody, so lovely it brought tears to her eyes, drifted out over the altar and seemed to wrap its message around her heart. At first she thought it was a saxophone, but the tone was different from any instrument she'd ever heard. She could not imagine what combination of instruments would be capable of producing such a sound. The melody was more intricate and, at the same time simpler, than earthly music. Then the playing stopped, but the music remained—in Simone's soul, as if it had lit a candle that still burned there, like the one she carried with her from the doorway. She looked around, trying to figure out where the music had been coming from—that was when she noticed a door behind the altar on the right side.

A ribbon of light was coming from under the door and she could see a flicker of movement. Someone was standing behind that fourth door—the someone who had been playing the music. She had to hear it again and see the musician who created it. As she watched, the ribbon of light grew larger. The door was opening.

The light from the little room was so bright in the dim sanctuary that Simone could not see the face of the person standing inside. She could only see the outline of a tall figure who held an instrument that glowed golden as flames of fire. Then the person stepped out of the room and she could see clearly that this was an angel of

22
♪

biblical description: wings, a glowing robe, shining hair with an aura that could only be described as a halo. Whether it was a man or a woman was unclear—it was beautiful in a way that was above the idea of masculine or feminine. The angel held a musical instrument that looked like it had been carved from an animal's horn—maybe that was what a ram's horn looked like—and embellished with gold piping and valves. He or she held out the instrument to Simone and spoke, or maybe just sent the words to her mind without speaking: "Will you take it? This belongs to you."

Simone took a step toward the heavenly instrument, her heart pounding so loudly she could hear it pulsing in her ears. She had never desired anything as strongly in her life as to play music like the piece she had just heard. As she began to lift her hands to receive it, the whole scene began to shimmer and fell away like a waterfall.

Next thing she knew she found herself sitting up in her own bed. The sound of her heart hammering against her ribs was now the only sound she could hear in the darkness of her own room. She sighed and laid her head back down on her pillow, trying to gather the details of the dream and keep them in her conscious memory. But almost every element of the dream faded as she tried to capture it, like waves lapping sand on a beach and disappearing back into the ocean. She would only be able to remember something about an angel playing music and a series of doors, until she began to dream it again some other night.

4

Lunch Quiz

"DO YOU DREAM in color?" Michelle asked the lunch group. She was checking off answers to questions in a magazine survey. It was pizzaburger day, so everyone had finished devouring that favorite lunch item way before the bell. They were all just sitting there feeling stuffed and wanting to relax before they split up for their next classes.

"I do," said Angela. "Last night I dreamed my hair was red like my aunt's."

"Which aunt? They both have red hair," Michelle asked.

"Is that in the survey?" Kyle smirked and pushed his large glasses back up his nose.

"Of course not," Michelle said in an authoritative voice. "It's not a survey about your family; it's about cre-

24

ativity. It shows how imaginative you are. Five is the highest score per question, and you get a 5 if you dream in color. There are a bunch of questions about dreams here. That makes sense. You probably have more elaborate dreams if you are a creative . . ."

Simone had been staring into space, ignoring the survey conversation until she heard this. "Does it say anything about having dreams but not being able to remember them?" she asked.

"Well, if you can't remember your dream, how do you know you had one?" Kyle asked before Michelle could answer Simone's question.

"I mean, maybe you could only remember part of a dream," Simone said, blushing, as everyone suddenly looked her way.

"Oh, that is annoying," said a voice behind Kyle. They all turned their heads the opposite direction to see who had spoken. It was Madame Corbeau, their French teacher. The petite older lady had a very concerned look on her face. As she stood there holding a plastic lunch tray, her clear blue eyes focused intently on Simone. "Sorry, I wasn't eavesdropping—I just happened to hear you say something about remembering dreams as I walked by. I just hate it when I can only remember part of the story. It's as if my subconscious is trying to tell me something, but the call gets dropped, *n'est-ce pas?*"

"That's exactly what it's like," Simone agreed. "I feel like I'm supposed to know something, to remember something, but I can't. As soon as I wake up, it all fades

25

♪

away. But I know I've been meeting people and a lot of things have happened. It's like I have a whole other life or something."

"Exactly," Madame said, nodding as if she knew just what Simone meant. "But dreams when you are sleeping are usually all wrapped up in the dreams you have for yourself when you are awake. Your dreams are symbols of your hopes and goals in your waking life."

"Wow! That's more interesting than just figuring out if you're creative or not," said Michelle, closing the magazine. "Do you know what it means when you dream you're flying?"

"I don't think the question is whether I know what it means." The silver-haired teacher smiled gently, her eyes twinkling. "The question is, do you know what that means to your dreaming mind? Everyone is different. For some people, flying means freedom or some kind of positive adventure. To others, it can symbolize being out of control and on the verge of falling."

"I dream about flying a lot," said Kyle. "I don't know if it stands for freedom or losing control."

"Oh, I bet it means freedom to you," Angela said. "You like adventure, Kyle. You don't lose your head when things get out of control. I remember how you ran toward danger when we faced it at the cottage—even though you didn't have any idea how it was going to turn out."

Kyle looked at his friend and felt grateful she'd been left with that impression. To tell the truth, he had been ter-rified when strange supernatural things started happening

26

there. It was one thing to face a kidnapper and another to confront a fallen angel—a demon who planned to kill human beings without remorse. Kyle had always thought faith was interesting to discuss at church, but he never imagined going into battle with it. For him their adventure had opened a door into the supernatural that could never again be closed. He now knew angels and demons were real and there was war going on between them. Faith was one of the only weapons that would help if they got caught in the middle of that war.

Madame Corbeau, still talking about dreams, pointed to Angela. "Now there's a good way to find out about your dream symbols. If you aren't sure what they mean, ask someone who knows you well. Sometimes those who are closest to you can tell you a lot about yourself."

With that the bell rang and they all started gathering up their things to go to class. Everyone except Simone. She sat there, staring into space again, wondering if anyone knew her well enough to tell her about her dream's symbols—the few she could remember. She'd led a double life for so long, half her life was in secrecy and half in the spotlight. Her mom knew her better than anyone—Simone didn't have to keep secrets *from* her, she just had to keep secrets *with* her. Mom would know what to say about her dreams. If only . . . Simone finally looked up and was surprised to see Madame Corbeau still standing there quietly.

"A penny for your thoughts?" she offered, looking at the girl kindly.

"Oh, I was just thinking about dreams and all. It's an interesting subject," Simone said, trying to look unconcerned.

"And a puzzle for you to solve?" the teacher asked.

Simone looked into Madame's wise eyes and at the all-too-knowing expression on her face. Was she talking about what she had just heard about Simone's mysterious dream, or did she know something? Something that could be dangerous to Simone and her family?

"Well, it's probably nothing, just a silly dream," Simone said, stuffing her papers and books into her back-pack and hoping the teacher had a class to hurry off to or would get the hint that Simone needed to go. She remembered her mom's rule about people with idle curiosity—don't confirm or deny their suspicions—that was the best way to discourage them. She had learned how to reply so she didn't say yes or no if someone was trying to guess at an answer.

"Our dreams aren't silly, whether they are the waking or sleeping variety. They should not be taken lightly," Madame told her and patted her shoulder before going on her way.

Simone watched her go. She didn't need anyone to tell her about her waking dreams and goals—they hounded her all day long. And she just knew if she worked hard enough, she'd soon have a chance to make them come true.

5

Boy Band

NO OTHER LUNCH *can beat pizzaburgers*, Adam thought as he strode down the hall to the band room with a satisfied smile. He felt full but not sleepy, though he moved slowly, his mammoth bari sax case slung over one shoulder and a loaded backpack of books over the other to balance it out.

"Hey, wide load, move it," someone yelled from behind, jostling the case so it fell from Adam's shoulder. He caught it just as the strap reached his elbow, but the heavy bag swung around, throwing him off balance. He bumped into several other students near him, setting off cries of "Watch it!" and "Hey, look out!" all around.

Dirty looks were not the only consequence. "Band geek! What's the matter, not strong enough to carry your flute, boy?" Tom Bannon mocked as he gave Adam a meaty forearm. Tom seemed to think it was part of his duty as a football player to heckle band members. Lots of the guys on the team were friendly with the bandies, but Tom and several others went out of their way to bother Adam about leaving the team to play music. Great. Could there be a worse person to bump into?

"Sorry, Tom," Adam said, looking down at the guy from a six-inch height advantage as he repositioned his case. Why did this guy try to pick a fight with him every chance he got? It wouldn't be fair to take out someone smaller than himself. Adam felt an almost nauseating surge of adrenaline grip his body—fight or flight? He prayed silently, "God, help me."

"Chicken! Prance along to your music lesson. You don't want to be late for your girlfriend." Tom tilted his head toward the band room door where Simone was standing. Adam chuckled. He didn't really care if anyone thought Simone was his girlfriend, but the idea of her hearing that accusation made him laugh—she'd probably explode. Man, Tom would find himself in much greater danger crossing Simone than someone bigger!

The laugh broke his tension and Adam just shrugged and let it go. Who cared what that jerk thought? The guy had barely made the cut for football, so he was probably jealous that Adam had had a choice.

But Tom's comment made him wonder . . . Did people think he was more than friends with Simone? He couldn't imagine she'd ever think of him that way . . . but maybe he was missing something! He looked at her scowling at a poster by the doorway. She had the prettiest frown dimples.

"What's up, Simone?" he asked to get her attention. "Hey, want to hear something funny? Tom just said . . ."

"No, I'm not in the mood for jokes," she said, raising one hand like a traffic cop. "Look at this poster. It's got some new details about the band competition that weren't on the form I filled out." She looked around to see if anyone else was listening, then lowered her voice and pointed to one line. "It says the judges are going to be from Glittering Genius record label."

"So?"

"That's terrible news. They only sign 'boy bands' or female vocalists with no last name. I can't believe a prestigious college like Centre d'Etudes would allow them to have the final choice. It's hopeless. We're never going to win."

Her face looked so desperate. He knew the contest was important to her. From what she'd told him, Simone was hoping it would give her a chance to see her mom. The winning band would get a music scholarship and a free trip to the record label's European headquarters in Paris. Her mom had been working on a book there for weeks and wouldn't be able to come home for months. If their band won, they'd get a scholarship to study at Centre d'Etudes in Paris next semester and learn the recording business from professionals. Two of Simone's dreams would come true at once. But Adam didn't know he had only heard half the story.

31

"Don't give up so easily," he said, putting on his most confident expression for her. "Colleges are like every other business, they like famous people to put their names and faces behind their school. I'm sure someone more musically qualified is the real judge and those guys are just involved for publicity. Our band has the most unique sound around. A real pro will hear that. You'll find out when we play at The Main Stage on Saturday. C'mon. Let's get to class."

Simone tried to feel encouraged, but she had a certain funny feeling again—one she had felt many times before. Maybe it was just because she thought Adam was trying to be more encouraging than he really felt. At least, she hoped that was the reason.

They walked through the door to the band room and took their places next to each other in the sax section. Simone busily put her horn together and watched Adam out of the corner of her eye. Nothing seemed unusual, but she had learned to be careful and wait to see if her strange feeling would turn out to be a warning.

Adam and the rest of the school believed Simone's mom worked for a company that published books and magazines about travel and history. That was her cover story and it was what Simone had believed, too, until she got old enough to start asking more serious and specific questions about her mom's job and the business trips that took her all over the world.

She found out the truth one afternoon when she came home early from a junior high soccer game and overheard her parents' private conversation. They were talking in a way that sounded like they were fighting. Simone stopped short of opening the garage door into the kitchen because it startled her. She'd almost never heard them disagree. The two of them took the expression "united front" to the extreme. It sounded a little scary to hear them take an angry tone with each other. She thought she'd go around to the front door and make some noise to let them know she was home, but when she heard her own name mentioned, she couldn't help waiting to hear what they were saying.

"We have to tell Simone," her mom said. "She's asking a lot of questions, and she'll know if I lie to her. She's like me, Stephen. She has the same gift."

"She's too young," Dad said firmly. Even though she couldn't see him, Simone imagined her dad was standing up as straight, as he often did when making an important statement. His thin figure reminded her of an exclamation mark when he did that. Then he'd push up his wire-rimmed glasses that were always sliding down his long nose. She thought he looked his part as a college professor, with his dark, serious eyes, somewhat disheveled hairstyle, and thrown-together clothing ensembles that usually included a weathered sweater of some kind. "Mandy, wait until she's through with high school, then she can know. When it's time for her to pick a college and a major, knowing what you really do could come in handy. If she's as talented as you are, she'll want to think about her options."

"That'll be too late," Mom said. "They are ruining her intuition already. She knows when someone is telling the truth and when someone is lying. It's the same as it was for me at her age. We can't let her start doubting her gift. It's like trying to play an out-of-tune piano. If enough people tell a musician her ear is wrong, even though she can hear that an instrument isn't tuned correctly, they will talk her out of her ability."

"So you think people are already telling her she is imagining things when she questions them because she thinks they're lying? I don't see how they'd get away with that."

"That's because you haven't experienced it. There is nothing worse than knowing the truth and having everyone around you deny it." Mom's foot tapped the floor impatiently. Even though her mom was a good twelve inches shorter than Dad, she was feisty. Her joke was to stand up to him "toe-to-toe" and shake her head so her curly, black ponytail swished back and forth. But the tone in her voice that day was no joke.

"Honey, I'm sorry," Dad said. "I guess being a human lie detector must be pretty scary sometimes."

A human lie detector? *What does that mean?* Simone felt like shouting. Then she realized she knew exactly what it meant. So maybe she wasn't going crazy! If she understood what they were talking about, a lot of things she'd been going through suddenly all made sense. She had thought she was just developing a suspicious nature— her friends had started telling her to lighten up. But she couldn't help noticing that when she had that certain feeling about whether she could believe what she had been told, events seemed to play out in a way that showed her she had been right to distrust what had been said. Just that day her friend Kelly had admitted she'd been making up an excuse to get out of class when she told the teacher she was sick. Somehow Simone had known as soon as she heard it. At first she explained the weirdness to herself by thinking Kelly was just a bad liar and everyone knew. Later, she found out that excuse wouldn't work—Kelly's act had fooled everyone except Simone.

"Well, it's only scary when you don't understand what's happening to you," Mom said, calming down a little. "I have to talk to her."

That's an entrance line if I ever heard one, Simone thought. She bustled noisily through the door, saying as casually as she could, "Talk to me about what?"

"Okay, it's your call, Mandy," Dad said and nodded to Mom.

"Come on in and sit with us," Mom said. She gave Simone a hug and Dad sat down and made room for them next to him on the couch.

And that was when they had the talk. Probably the most important talk of her life so far. Afterward, Simone understood why her parents had wanted to wait to explain everything to her.

35
♪

"My side of the family has passed down something more rare than musical talent," Mom began. "Or maybe it's just part of having a musical 'ear' or hearing correctly. It's nothing weird, just a talent—though it seems to be a rare one, like having perfect pitch. I often wonder, though, if it's more common than we know and people are simply talked out of it before they have a chance to let it develop. Anyway, I have seen some signs it might have been passed on to you, and I don't want you to get scared or confused about it if that's the case."

Tell me already! Simone's thoughts screamed. She was pretty sure she knew what her mom was going to say. At least, she hoped she knew.

"This isn't easy to describe, but the best explanation is that some people are like human lie detectors—they can tell whether someone is telling the truth beyond just suspecting the information to be false or reading the speaker's body language. When I was your age, I thought I was going crazy because I'd have this feeling—stronger than a gut feeling or intuition—so strong it was almost like a taste in my mouth when someone was not telling the truth."

Simone's stomach did flip-flops and her heart raced. *She knows! Mom knows that feeling!*

She was so excited she grabbed her mom's hands and said, "So that's why I keep having these weird feelings about what people are saying. I thought I was getting paranoid or something. But then afterward things keep happening that prove they were lying, and I just about lose it. I haven't been able to tell anyone. They'd think I'm imagining things. I've never heard of such a thing."

"Oh, my poor child," Mom said, putting her arms around Simone. "I'm afraid I've waited too long to tell you."

"But what else could you do?" Dad said. "If you told her too soon and she didn't have the talent, she might imagine she did and get even more confused."

"Yes, I was waiting for you to prove it to yourself," Mom said with a sigh.

Simone was both relieved and confused. This one answer, that she'd thought could solve everything, seemed only to lead to more questions. She hugged her mom back, and then said, "I guess you were right about waiting until I noticed something was going on. If you'd told me before I began to have these experiences, I don't know if I'd have believed you. It's not a talent I've heard of in school or anything. But, Mom, if this is really true, people lie all the time! Even 'good' people. Even my friends! How can you live with this, Mom? Isn't it better not to know—just let people have their secrets and tell you whatever they want? I mean it's not like you haven't got secrets to keep yourself!"

"I do," said Mom with a sigh. "And that's something else we need to talk about. Simone, I've never lied to you about what I do for a living. You've seen the magazine articles with my name in the byline. But the magazine itself is more than it appears to be. It has a more serious

37
♪

purpose than just to inform people about good deals on vacations and business travel. I can't tell you everything, but I won't lie to you. I'll tell you the truth about everything I can talk to you about."

And that was when she found out her mom was a secret agent. It was so unlikely, Simone had to chuckle every time she thought about it. Mom was the least suspicious person you'd ever meet. She never got searched at airports or questioned when she presented her passport. Her sweet expression and genuine warmth led people to trust her the moment they met her. In a way it made sense. If you were going to choose someone to be a secret agent, wouldn't you really want a person who looked the least like one, instead of some glamorous person who'd attract attention and be remembered? The movies had got that all wrong, according to Mom.

"Everyone I work with looks like your average tourist—we go out of our way to look 'forgettable' rather than interesting. When we write a story about a new restaurant or do research for a book about the history of a city, it gives us a cover story so we can go to places where our help is needed without arousing suspicion from the enemy."

"What enemy? Whom are you spying on? Who is it you really work for? The FBI? The CIA?" Simone asked.

"That's top secret, honey, sorry," was all Mom could say. "Just know that the world is a safer place because of all we do. A few very good people put their lives in danger and search out the truth, so many other good people

can live in peace. And, Simone, you have to remember—
I'm trusting you to keep my secret safe."

"Are you saying I should lie about what I know?"
Simone asked, confused. What good was a gift of truth if
it made your life into a lie?

"I don't want you to lie about it, but you can't tell
the secret side of what I do, either. It would put a lot of
people in danger, including our family. If your friends,
teachers, neighbors, or strangers ask you questions that
could lead to this secret being revealed, you have to
change the subject or not answer. It's a lot like the way
some people I interview for the magazine don't confirm
my suspicions, but they don't deny them, either. They
know I might eventually find out the facts they can't
reveal, and they don't want to be caught in a lie if I do.
They just refuse to comment and hope I'll move on and
ask them about something they *can* talk about."

"It's a funny world that way, now that I think about
it," Dad said. "People think they have to give an answer
just because someone is asking, but maybe that's why
there is so much lying. We should feel free to ignore a
question that's too personal or one that we just don't feel
like answering. Maybe when people feel cornered into
responding to something that they aren't supposed to talk
about, a lie seems their only out."

Was there something Dad couldn't talk about? Had
he been keeping a secret, too? Simone had to know.
"What about you, Dad? If Mom's a secret agent, what
do you really do, Mister? And don't even think about

39

lying to me now that I know I'm a human lie detector, too!"

It turned out she had one normal parent, at least. "I'm really just a boring old history prof. Outside of helping hold down the fort while your mom is out saving the world, I don't do anything all that exciting," he said with a smirk. That was a relief, because she didn't feel like processing any more surprises. Her dad was her rock, always home by dinner and available at his little closet of a college office for emergencies when Mom was traveling. He'd wait up for her or Mom, turning on every light in the house, or maybe just forgetting to turn them off without Mom to follow him around to do it.

40
♪

Her friend Adam reminded Simone of Dad that way—he was another rock in her muddy world. She looked at him sitting a few seats away and smiled. She knew she could count on Adam to help, so he was the first person she'd talked with about most of her plan—all the details of the plan she could freely tell outside the family.

6

Road Trip

S ATURDAY CAME so fast that Simone checked her cell phone calendar twice the night before to make sure she hadn't skipped a day or two. But here she was loading her music and a small travel bag into Adam's dad's SUV. The first road trip for her band would be a real milestone, but it had felt more like a *millstone* around her neck for several weeks as they rehearsed for it.

She had to admit the progress they'd made in such a short time was unbelievable. Knowing each other from band competition had helped, but their ability to "talk" to each other, to have a musical conversation as they played, was amazing. They just clicked. They were ready.

She slid onto the middle seat next to Adam and fastened her seat belt—good and tight, so the butterflies in her stomach wouldn't lift her off the seat. She decided not to think about where they were headed, and started day-dreaming about how they'd all met.

The whole idea of starting her own band had happened two months earlier, after she hit a dead end in a conversation with her dad. Back then it seemed as if everything was sliding into the lowest valley. Her mom had called home from Paris to say her latest research trip for a book on French youth hostels had turned into an "extended assignment." After several mysterious phone conversations, Simone realized she and her dad weren't going to find out any more information from Mom until she came home and could tell them in person.

   "Simone, you know better than to ask a lot of questions over the phone—Mom always says it's impossible to trust a phone to be secure," Dad said in reply to Simone's questions. But knowing Mom would be gone months, and not knowing why, was a strain for both Simone and her dad. Dad said, "All we can do is be patient and wait. We'll hear more from Mom at the right time." He smiled and put his arms around Simone, but she could see the worry lines form at the corners of his eyes. Every night he left almost every light in the house on until he went to bed. She knew that meant he was watching for Mom to suddenly show up at the door, her secret mission complete. Then he could say what he always said when she scolded him about wasting electricity: "I just wanted you to know we were expecting you."
   Although Dad's nightly ritual was sweet, it also made Simone sad to see him shuffle off to bed alone. She

decided she had to try to do something about it. When
she heard about the music contest, it seemed like the perfect solution. She thought she had a chance of winning
the trip to Paris. Surely Dad wouldn't object if she just
happened to win a free supervised trip to the right place
at the right time.

At first Simone's plan was just to get there and make
sure her mom was okay. One of the only things she could
remember about her recurring dream was a sense of danger, and Simone felt sure it had something to do with her
mom—sure that Mom needed help and was unable to
tell them directly.

The second thing that convinced her of this was that
her dad was lying about it.

Well, he was *probably* lying. She couldn't always trust
her inherited "truth detector." She'd sometimes get a "lie
flash" when someone was just trying to put a brave face
on things. If the person didn't know for sure something
would go the way he hoped, or if he wanted to encourage her about the possibility of a good outcome, she'd get
"that lying feeling". She felt it big time whenever her dad
told her to be patient and not to worry.

"There's no reason to worry. Just pray for Mom. She
knows how to do her job," he said with that patient look
Simone both envied and hated. It meant the conversation
wasn't going anywhere near revealing new information
about Mom's situation. It meant Dad was satisfied there
was nothing for them to do about it—that Mom was in
the hands of the intelligence community and the Lord.
Maybe not in that exact order. Dad trusted God with

43
♪

everything. Almost every inquiry—intellectual, personal, or factual—could be broken down into "That's in God's hands" if followed to Dad's ultimate conclusion.

To Simone, that sounded like giving up, and her truth detector told her that, in his heart, he wasn't as sure about the situation as his brave words would have her believe.

"Dad, waiting on God is not always enough. There is a time for action—when you just have to use the brains God has given you and take care of things!" Simone was sure the time had come. Adam had encouraged her and, honestly, if he hadn't helped she might never have done it. She looked over at him sitting next to her in the car and smiled, remembering his words and his actions were responsible for the band being on the road to their first gig together.

"Well, of course you want to see your mom," Adam had said when she told him as much of her plan to enter the contest as she could. "Your dad's not going to say no if you win the scholarship. He'll be proud of you. What about your mom? Are you going to tell her?"

"I'll just surprise her IF we win. That's a big *if* right now. I think that's why Dad didn't have any objections to my entering the contest. He knows it's a long shot . . . and he probably thinks it will keep me busy so I won't have time to worry." Simone couldn't tell Adam that they hadn't actually spoken with her mom for 2 weeks. She desperately wanted to confide in someone, but she didn't want to make the situation worse by letting out Mom's secret now.

"Okay, Simone, if we don't want to let everyone at school know about your plan, maybe we should pick musicians from some other high school. How about those three guys from Paul Revere High we met at regionals? Remember, they were so excited about starting a jazz ensemble, but needed saxophone players?"

Simone nodded and smiled. She still had their phone numbers in her planner and they were just the three she had been thinking of. Adam was the right person to confide in—he always seemed to be on the same page—and this confirmed both the decision to include him and her intuition about the players she needed. Conan, Greg, and Moby had been practicing together since junior high, and they'd shown off their skill as a trio at a regional competition last spring. Simone and Adam felt flattered when Greg asked if they'd consider playing together sometime.

"I know where to find them without calling," Adam said mysteriously. "Meet me after school and I'll take you where those guys show off their hidden talents."

He was waiting in the parking lot after last bell and held open the door to the new black Kia his parents had just given him for his sixteenth birthday. He refused to tell Simone where they were going. "Are they playing a gig around here?" she asked.

"You'll see. I have a few secrets of my own, you know." He wouldn't tell her anything else until they were near Paul Revere High. He unexpectedly turned off the

45

♪

road into the parking lot of a coffee shop that had a sign over the front door with the name "Taste of Heaven" painted in dainty teal letters next to two chubby angels. Simone guessed Adam wanted to pick up a drink before they met the guys. He spun into the drive-thru lane of the quaint little place, making a lot of noise with his tires, and then honked loud and long twice. Shocked by this sort of rudeness, completely unlike Adam, Simone blushed and scooted down in her seat, expecting trouble. Suddenly, a head full of blond dreadlocks popped out the window and the owner yelled, "Wait your turn!" It was Moby.

"Oh, hey, Adam," he said, relaxing his angry scowl into a grin. "C'mon in, man." He waved them through the drive-thru lane, pointing to the parking around back.

Simone laughed as they got out of the car. "Oh, so this is where they show off their hidden talents, huh?"

"You'll see" was Adam's only reply.

They opened the door to the little shop and wonderful smells poured out: fresh-brewed coffee, vanilla, cinnamon, chocolate, and lots of other flavors that had been trapped behind the glass door as if sealed inside a potpourri bottle. And then they saw the guys they'd previously only seen in band competition tuxes, wearing the usual gear baristas in hippie coffee shops wore: bandanas and black canvas aprons over white tees and jeans. Moby's bandana looked like it had slipped off to one side and he'd probably tried to retie it without a mirror. It had turned into a headband that didn't prevent his dreads from escaping, as it was no doubt supposed to do.

46
♪

Simone imagined this wardrobe malfunction "accidentally" happened every day, as Moby leaped over the swinging counter gate in a bound and greeted them with free-spirited hugs.

Greg and Conan were twin brothers and they looked it, like mirror images of each other in their coffee shop gear. They both leaned across the coffee counter and slapped palms with Adam, then shook Simone's hand with more decorum.

"Ah, the lovely Adam and the brilliant Simone," Greg cooed. "Will you join us for a sip of heaven?" Conan swept his arm out to indicate the only large corner booth, and they all sat. Moby brought a steaming coffee pot balanced on a tray beside five rather dainty, flowered coffee cups and saucers.

"Simone?" Greg asked as he placed a cup and saucer in front of her and poised the coffee pot above it, ready to pour.

"What is it?" Simone asked. It seemed odd they'd have a pot ready to go at a moment's notice. Even odder that the china pot matched the floral cups and saucers. It looked like it belonged in some elderly lady's kitchen instead in a coffee shop.

"It's Grandma's Blueberry Koffee," Adam said, pointing to the menu where the name of the coffee was illustrated in large letters. He seemed ready to salivate as he held up his cup.

Moby smiled encouragingly and passed around a silver tray with sugar and cream. "Try a drop."

47
♪

"Okay. Just a little. I don't really drink coffee."

"It's our grandma's special blend. Even people who don't drink coffee like it. All organic ingredients. It's practically all we brew here. Once they've tried it, customers rarely ask for anything else," Conan said, his expression suggesting he was offering a special treat.

Simone stirred in a lot of cream and sugar. "Your grandma's cups?"

"Of course," Greg said, laughing. "You don't think we'd pick these out on our own, do you?"

"Do you?" echoed Conan, looking a bit distressed.

"Naw, of course not," Adam said, smacking him on the shoulder.

"We're just keeping the place running the way Grandma would have—in memory of her, you know?" Greg explained. "She left it to us because we'd helped her after school and knew all about the business. Grandma raised us as much as our parents did. She was great."

Conan turned over the menu and pointed to a photo of a gray-haired lady holding one of the fancy coffee cups. Under the picture, it said, "Grandma Heaton and her famous Blueberry Koffee."

Simone tasted the coffee and smiled. Blueberries, cream, sugar, and just a hint of chocolate accented the coffee flavor. It was like chocolate blueberry pie. "Now I'm ruined for all other coffee," she said to the guys' delight. "But we didn't come here to mooch your coffee. We want to know if you were serious about your offer to play together. I need a band."

That got their attention away from coffee and Moby quickly answered for all of them. "We're on board. We've been talking about this ever since we met you two. You have a gig?"

"Not a paying one—not right away—but if we win, it'll pay off big time," Adam said.

He pulled a wrinkled entry form from his pocket and smoothed it out next to the coffee pot on the table. The three guys passed it around and nodded, asked a few questions, and the deal was struck. "We're in." They decided to name the band after the coffee they'd been drinking when they got together. Blueberry Koffee was born.

Simone would never have guessed how well it would all go. Now the five band members looked around at each other as they drove together. No one could believe this day was finally here. "Pinch me," Moby said to Simone, holding out his hand. "Ouch!" he squealed, and everyone laughed and imitated him.

"You scream like a girl," Conan said.

They headed south, following a map they'd been sent in an information package from the contest, toward a venue in Nelsonville, Ohio, listed as The Main Stage. The long drive would take most of the day and there wasn't room for Greg, Conan, and Moby's "groupies" to ride along.

"Don't worry about a thing," Doug Wembly, the public relations guy from the contest, had told Simone and Adam over the phone. "A judge from the contest will

49

meet you there and arrange rooms for you all nearby. The next day you drive to the other side of the state to play at The College Corner, near the Ohio and Indiana border. Local judges we've hired will listen to your live performance both days. If you get a score in the top 10 percent of the bands playing, you'll play again to enter the final round."

Simone got a definite "lie flash" as she listened. She wondered if she should ask to talk to Wembly's supervisor or something. She muted the phone and told Adam. "He sounds shady. I don't believe him."

"He's a PR guy," Adam said with a shrug. "One step down from a telemarketer—he'll say anything to get the job done. Do you want to back out?"

Simone shook her head and unmuted the cell. "Uh, give me phone numbers for the judges, so we can arrange to meet."

"Okay, I'll call you back with them. I'm in my car. Listen, sweetie, you just get your end of things going. I'll take care of everything on this end. You're going to be glad you did this. Even if you don't win, the free publicity for your band will be great. Radio spots, newspaper spots, and both venues I've scheduled you for are near colleges where we advertise, so you'll have plenty of students in the audience. You can't buy publicity like that."

Wembly had not called back, but he'd e-mailed her the time and addresses where they were to perform, saying the judges would meet them there. Adam said the guy sounded like a busy go-fer with bigger performers to worry about and they should just go. Everyone agreed. Now all they had to do was drive and drive. Highway 77 was interesting because it passed through many of the familiar towns that make up the Cleveland area. They'd visited schools in those towns for football games and band competitions and had stories to tell about each place. By the time they turned south on 71, however, it was just a lot of flat freeway without anything new in the way of scenery or towns they knew about.

Every half hour or so, to break the monotony, someone said "Pinch me" and squealed. Moby got sick of being the brunt of their joke and threw a shoe at Greg. Everyone wished he hadn't taken it off and took turns moaning as they tossed the gamey shoe around the car.

"Oh, man, that's gross."

"Did you wash your socks in cheese sauce about a week ago?"

"No, it's fish . . . there's a dead fish in there. Smell this."

"No, get it outta here."

"It's not as bad as mine," said Conan. "Here, Simone, smell this one. Aren't mine worse?"

Simone gagged. Really. Her first "tour" with a band was not starting out to be as glamorous as she'd pictured. Being the only girl had its disadvantages, she decided. Competing for who smelled worse was a game she and her girlfriends would never think of playing. She was relieved when the guys said they were hungry and pulled off at an exit to look for fast food. She just wanted some fresh air.

51

7

One Ring

BACK IN TOWN, Marti felt like she needed fresh air, too, but for a different reason. She was relieved to finally get excused from her parents' counseling session.

Her mom and dad had been meeting with Pastor and Mrs. Grace a couple of times a week at the office overlooking the riding arena at Grace Barn. Marti had to attend at least one weekly session, where Mr. Grace kept asking in his most understanding voice, "And how does it make you feel to hear that, Marti?" It was nice to be asked, she guessed, after almost never being asked in the past. Her mom and dad's conversations were so strained they must have wanted to spare her the stress; unfortunately, that left her on the outside of important family decisions until after the fact. But the sessions were grueling, listening to her parents' complicated marriage problems and trying to have an opinion about them. "I wish they'd just get along," she answered.

James Grace was a gentle counselor and his flourishing silver beard made her think of Santa Claus. Not the commercial Santa on TV ads at Christmas, but a real Saint Nicholas as she pictured him from history, the one who gave presents to poor children and told them stories. He had a laugh that came straight from his heart at just the right moment in a conversation. His wife, Sara, had been Marti's riding instructor since Marti was a little girl, so it was also comforting to have Sara there. Sara mainly sat in her squeaky rocking chair that chirped like a cricket every now and again, listening and nodding, petting the silver tiger cat that followed her everywhere. Sara's calm gray eyes urged the person speaking to continue, no matter how painful the subject.

After almost an hour, Mr. Grace finally told Marti she could go to the barn while he talked with her parents some more. She didn't hesitate.

Lorena Philips watched her daughter through the big glass window as she rushed across the arena to the stables. "Pastor James, I'm concerned about Marti. She had a bad experience with Clé—we all did. I still shudder to think what might have happened without our friends' help. And Marti had just begun showing interest in dating. I guess she's a late bloomer in that way. By the time I was fifteen,

I'd been dating for two years . . ." Lorena began to have a faraway look in her eye, as if remembering.

Her husband broke in, sounding somewhat irritated. "Now there's this guy Billy Joe who's brought her home on his motorcycle several times. He's definitely interested in her, though she says he's just a friend. I understand he works for you here at the barn. Should I be concerned about him?"

James Grace shifted in his worn leather chair that creaked like an old saddle whenever he moved. He smiled reassuringly and said, "Billy Joe is one of the nicest boys you'll ever meet, even though he and his brother had a rough childhood. But I wouldn't trust him, or any other boy, with my daughter without having a good understanding about dating first. Let's talk about your expectations. Paul, what are your goals in allowing your daughter to date?"

"Goals? Well, we just want her to be a normal teenager. Dating is what kids her age do for fun. We aren't thinking ahead to marriage yet."

"Goodness, no!" Lorena gasped as if the thought were shocking.

Sara Grace spoke up now. "But why should thinking ahead to marriage be an amazing thing? Every investment you make for your child comes with potential. If you enroll her in riding lessons, you assess whether her goal will be to show horses or trail ride for fun. When she starts high school, you think ahead to where she will go to college and what major she could choose."

"Yes," agreed Pastor James. "It's wise to look at each new life step as the beginning of a race. Runners aren't just hurrying aimlessly along the course—there's a destination, a purpose. Teens often don't think of setting goals. They tend to react to situations as they happen, so an important of part of parenting is helping them understand they are making decisions that will affect the rest of their lives. I think we all remember our first crush—whether positive or negative—even though years have passed."

Lorena stared at him a moment. Had he guessed the thoughts she was just having about her own teenage experiences with dating? She blushed. "Well, everyone has negative experiences. You know what they say . . . you have to kiss a lot of frogs before you find your prince." She patted her husband's hand, but he frowned at her.

"Is that supposed to be a comforting thought about Marti? I don't want her kissing anyone. I don't care how young you started dating. This is our little girl you're talking about, for heaven's sake!"

Sara Grace asked a question to smooth out the conflict, a small smile forming at the corners of her lips. "Well, do you think there is a middle ground you two can find between letting Marti date at random and not letting her out of her room?"

Lorena looked defensive. "Well, sure, I'd like to give my daughter advice about dating. It's just that it isn't easy to get her to talk about, um, you know, that kind of thing—let alone get her to take any advice."

55
♪

"What are other parents doing about it? What about Angela's parents?" Paul asked.

Pastor James leaned back in the comfy chair and smiled. "Ah, that's a good question. Several of the families who go to church here got into doing some research a couple of years ago about biblical ways to address the subject. They wanted to talk to their kids about life goals, but not in a way that would make them the 'date police.' They hoped their teens would take responsibility for their own decisions, rather than just letting things happen and blaming the circumstances afterward."

Lorena looked hopeful. "Did they find something that worked?"

"They found a Christian family retreat to go to with their teens. The idea they brought back was about making a pledge to each other. The teens promised to choose to begin all their relationships with the opposite sex with the end goal of finding someone they could marry for life. That means they wouldn't date casually, just to go out, without considering whether the person would meet their standards for a spouse.

"They also promised to treat anyone they dated as they'd want everyone to treat the person they will ultimately marry—with respect and purity. The parents promised to support that goal by being there to help them achieve it in any way they could. That includes talking about everything openly, with the promise not to overreact about what might be revealed in those talks."

Paul sighed and looked out the window at his daughter and her friend Angela, who were riding their horses around the sawdust ring. "Oh, man, that's scary! Don't you think grounding her until she's twenty-one would be easier?"

James gave one of his heartfelt laughs and patted Paul's shoulder. "Sure sounds like it. Want to try to see if you can get that to work for you?" That idea made everyone laugh.

Sara said, "Why don't you two talk with the Clarksons and see what you can find out about their experience? I'm sure they'd be happy to tell you; and they're not the kind who'd pressure you if you don't agree with what they think."

"That's a great idea," Lorena said. "I'm really afraid to take the risk that our daughter will get mad at us and think we are butting into her personal life. But now that I hear this, I wish someone would have taken the risk and given me this kind of direction before I started stumbling into dating."

She looked really sad and Paul put his arm around her. "Well, you managed to stumble into this frog and make him your prince, so it turned out okay in the end." Lorena smiled and the Graces looked at each other and did the same. They could see the troubled couple were making progress as they ended their session with a hug.

Marti glanced up to the office window every now and then as she rode Bobcat past, his hooves making soft thumps in the sawdust and sand mixture that padded the arena floor. The black pony snorted every time she looked away, complaining about her attention shift. He was so attuned to his rider's movements that he almost seemed to read her mind. She wished everyone were this easy to communicate with—especially her parents. She looked in the big mirror that spanned one wall of the arena to check her posture and was startled to see what a sad look her face held.

"What's the matter? Worried about your hair?" Angela teased as she passed her friend on the inside of the circle and gave her a playful tap on the elbow.

Marti's short hair was only visible at the edges of her black schooling helmet. "Yeah, right. I feel bad my hair doesn't match my horse's tail, like yours does."

"He's a blond and I'm a brunette, so I don't see what we have in common," Angela answered, patting the palomino horse.

"You both have pieces of straw stuck in your tails." Marti stopped her horse at the exit to the barn and dismounted. "I'm done. I just can't concentrate with everyone watching us." She walked her horse into the aisle of stalls where she cross-tied him and began taking off his tack.

Angela dismounted, and then followed, self-consciously shaking the straw out of her ponytail. "How's it going with your parents?"

"Well, things have really gotten better at home. I just don't like all the focus on me at these counseling things. I feel like a bug under a microscope. The Graces are nice and all that, but I'm used to being ignored, not quizzed about all my feelings. I'm not sure what I should say, and what to keep to myself. I'm not sure my parents could handle hearing what I'd answer if I told them *everything*! I mean, my dad looked like his head was going to pop off the first time Billy Joe came to pick me up on his motorcycle."

They both laughed. Angela wished she could have seen that. "I can't imagine what your dad thought about watching his little girl ride away on the back of that bike—with Billy Joe grinning like an idiot, no doubt. He always looks like he's up to something."

"Yes, even when he's not. He really is very polite, in spite of that "outlaw cowboy" look he's put together for himself."

"I wonder where he even finds that stuff in northern Ohio. He must do his clothes shopping at rodeos . . ."

"Angela, you're so lucky. I can tell your parents don't worry about Kyle. They don't seem to worry about anything."

"Kyle and I are just friends. And if that ever changes, I already have an understanding with my parents on things like that."

"What understanding?"

"They promised to *be* understanding; it's an agreement about dating and stuff."

"So what did you agree to do?"

Angela twisted the pretty silver ring she always wore on her left hand. "It wasn't just what *I* agreed to do; it was

59
♪

what *we* agreed to do as a family. See this ring? It's a promise ring. My dad gave it to me. It means that he, as well as Mom, pledged to be my protection. And I promised to let them protect me."

"How?"

"We went to a family camp where they helped us decide on some rules ahead of time for how to handle dates and things like that. It was easy to say yes after we talked about the things all of us really wanted to happen with that.

"The best part of it for me was when my parents agreed not to go crazy when I tell them I'm interested in someone romantically. The camp leaders really made a point that they had to promise that. So that makes it easy for me—or at least it will be easy someday—to be honest with them about what's going on between me and, uh, whoever. They've already agreed there will be a 'whoever,' so I don't have to worry about their reaction."

Marti looked at the silver ring. "It looks like a braid. So what did you tell them you 'want to happen' with this unknown guy?"

"The ring has three strands of silver woven together. They stand for my promise, my parents' promise, and God's promise. What I promised is that I won't date just to be 'social' or because everyone else is dating, but instead I'll have a higher purpose in mind. And not just for me, but for the guy, too."

"A higher purpose? So, what does that mean? All your dates are at church?" Marti laughed and threw a curry brush to her friend. Angela shook her head and scrubbed at some muddy spots on her horse's gold-colored flank.

"Nothing religious. It's just a practical view about relationships. I agreed I won't get into a serious relationship with anyone I wouldn't consider marrying someday."

"What! How can you possibly know if you'd marry someone when you first date him?"

"Well, I made a list."

Marti dropped the brush she'd been using and stared at Angela.

"So you have a questionnaire for guys?"

"No, not like that. But, be honest, don't you have an unwritten list of things you'd never tolerate in a guy? And another secret list of things he'd just have to be like for him to be interesting to you?"

Marti turned away for a minute, seeming to concentrate on digging through the toolbox for a different grooming brush. Her face felt like it was burning. Was she blushing? "Hmmm well, okay, I guess I do."

Angela smirked a "thought so" look aimed at Marti. "So after I admitted *that* to myself, my parents and I talked about what was on my list, and they suggested some things I could think about adding. Then we prayed for my future husband, wherever he is, that God would help him grow into the man I want to spend my life with."

"I can't believe it. You prayed for someone you've never met?"

61
♪

"Maybe. How do I know I've never met him? By the time I'm serious about marriage, someone I already know might have grown up into the man my list describes. What's important is what that prayer did for my outlook on guys."

"What's that?"

"Whenever I'm with a guy, I'm going to think about how I'd want a girl to treat the man I'll marry someday. I don't want him to have hurts or regrets to remember. I already love him, even though I probably haven't met him yet. That's how I'll think about a guy I date. I want the girl he finally marries to feel like thanking me for the way I treated her husband. And if I'm the girl he marries, I want to have good memories about how we started out together."

"Amazing." Marti turned around again for a minute. She was wiping tears from her eyes.

"What's wrong, Marti?"

"I wish my parents had known to do something like that for me."

8

Behind the Scenes

THE SUN WAS settling down low in the sky above the rural community of Nelsonville, Ohio, when Blueberry Koffee rolled into town. Inside the SUV, the aroma had a lot more going on than coffee, even though they had spilled plenty of it on the floor. The heater fan was circulating a mix of day-old T-shirt, funky tennis shoe, French fries, and soured creamer. They'd all decided Greg was the one wearing too much aftershave, even though he didn't look like he'd shaved.

Everyone was trying to give Moby directions from a series of maps and a few notes they had on a scrap of paper. "I can't use my laptop to find The Main Stage—there's no open wireless connection here. It's supposed to be on Washington Street," Adam said as he tapped the keyboard.

"Here! Here's Washington Street," Simone said, pointing to a sign ahead.

"Pull over!" Greg and Conan shouted at the same time.

Moby swerved to the curb next to an orange banner with bold green letters that spelled out "Harvest Hoedown." A balding man in an apron, carrying a huge tray of sweet corn, jumped as if he thought they were coming up onto the sidewalk.

Greg rolled down the window and they all tried to ask the man for directions at once. He stared at them a minute and then pointed to the right. They thanked him in a hoarse chorus and turned right at the Washington Street sign.

"This is not good," said Simone, looking at a large, open pavilion tent with a few people sitting around on folding lawn chairs. On a stage in the center of the canvas event tent, several little girls wearing scarecrow costumes were tap dancing to music played by an elderly man with a banjo and a recorded sound track.

Adam read aloud the large poster hanging over the street side of the pavilion as if to erase all doubt: "The Main Stage."

Moby parked at the curb and Greg slid out of his seat. "There's a schedule posted on that pole." He read it, pointed to it with his finger, and nodded glumly. "*Blueberry Koffee will be served up at seven o'clock.*"

"They didn't say it was an outdoor tent," Simone said.

"And we aren't really blueberry coffee," Adam said. "Hopefully, they know we're a band and don't think we're caterers."

"Though, now that I think of it, we have all the ingredients at Taste of Heaven. We could add catering to our list of band features if a venue wanted it," Greg said brightly. Too brightly. No one was in the mood for band marketing ideas after the long drive. Several socks, wrappers, and a bag of soggy French fries were flung his way from four directions as he tried to unload his bass case from the back of the car.

"It's already getting chilly out here," Simone said, hugging her bare arms and wishing she'd brought a coat. Simone hadn't dressed for being outside. She wore a light T-shirt, thinking of the hot lights the school band usually played under on indoor stages.

65
♪

Adam handed her his green hooded sweatshirt from the back of the car. "Isn't November sort of late in the season to be scheduling music outdoors?"

Southern Ohio obviously stayed a bit warmer than Cleveland, as they could see by the light sweaters the crowd wore—though you could hardly call it a "crowd" of people. A "sprinkling" of people maybe. A few lounged on lawn chairs eating candied apples and watching curiously as the band unpacked their gear.

The old banjo player finished playing for the miniature scarecrow girls, and several parents clapped and cheered. The gray-haired gentleman rose to his feet as the girls left the stage, smiled serenely, and nodded to the girls and their audience in appreciation. In a silken voice that sounded like a professional radio announcer's, he spoke into the microphone and immediately drew everyone's attention.

"Thank you so much, girls. That was so sweet. Can we give Miss Kim's Tapp-ettes another round of applause? That's great. Now we have a short intermission as we set up our next act. C'mon back in fifteen minutes and bring your friends. We have a real treat for you coming right up," he said, looking at Simone and company. "The Blueberry Koffee band is going to serve up some bluegrass in just a few minutes and you won't want to miss it."

He left the stage and walked slowly over to the car and held out his hand to Simone. She shook hands and immediately noticed his strong grip. She guessed it was from years of playing; and it just seemed logical that banjo playing would be quite a workout.

"Ed Cantor, at your service. You must be Simone, and you fellows are Blueberry Koffee, I presume?" The gray-bearded gentleman aimed his disarming smile first at Simone, then at the rest of the band. "What can I do to help you set up? We have electrical outlets here and you can use any of these amplifiers you'd like . . ." He swept his hand toward the stage and started walking in that direction.

"Thank you so much . . . uh . . . Excuse me," Moby stammered as he picked up his guitar case and followed Mr. Cantor. "Did you just announce we were playing *bluegrass* music?"

"Well, of course. When Wembly scheduled this he said your group is an exciting new sound in bluegrass."

Simone felt a chill in her gut, like she was going to be sick. How could Wembly lie about everything? Now they'd have to turn around and drive all the way home with nothing to show for their trouble. The disappointment seemed too much to bear.

"I'm sorry, Mr. Cantor. There seems to be some misunderstanding. Mr. Wembly knows we don't play bluegrass music. I'm afraid he's lied to both our group and you. We were told you knew we played jazz, that there would be a judge here from the scholarship contest, and that he'd arrange a place for us to stay overnight."

Mr. Cantor rubbed his beard and smiled. "Well, not everything is a lie. He did ask me to judge your group for the contest, and I've arranged for you all to stay at my home tonight. As for the style of music, I think we can work with that. You know, Nelsonville was once a very popular place with jazz musicians. We had some of the best "speakeasies" between Cleveland and Cincinnati in the 1930s."

67

♪

They all stared blankly at the old man and, finally, Moby asked, "What does that mean?"

"It means jazz, my young friend," Mr. Cantor said with a wink. "And when Prohibition ended, a lot of the musicians stayed and raised families here. When I was a boy, I grew up hearing some of the best musicians there were. I think you'll find I'm qualified to judge your contest entry. Yes, indeed. Now let's get you set up."

As he helped them get their equipment set up and plugged into the sound system, Mr. Cantor examined each instrument appreciatively, nodding and looking at each as if they were old friends, especially Simone's old saxophone. "A Selmer Mark VI, huh? Did you ever hear how some of these were made from recycled World War II shell casings? This is a real special vintage instrument."

He then disappeared for a few minutes while they did a sound check with a teenage boy in cowboy boots who urged them to hurry because he had to leave to go to the 4-H tent and "get a calf loaded."

"I didn't know calves were allowed to drink," Moby joked.

The boy just stared at him, then said, "Here comes Mr. Cantor. He'll finish up and run the board for you."

Mr. Cantor came back, and he wasn't alone this time. A group of a dozen men about his age were following him, talking together and laughing. Other people seemed to be drawn to the area or to the group of men, everyone calling out to others and gesturing as more people passed by. Suddenly, the audience area was filled and people were beginning to stand around the outside of the venue. When the band looked out over the crowd, it was like a sea of silver, as most of the people seemed to be Mr. Cantor's age. He had obviously put the word out to his friends within minutes of meeting the group.

The band members looked at each other. What was going on? Simone shrugged and smiled. It seemed hopeful, anyway. Mr. Cantor came up on the stage and motioned to Simone to step away from the microphone. "Okay, Simone, let's see your set list."

She showed him the entry sheet she'd filled out for the competition. They were only supposed to play three songs, so it wasn't much of a list. "We were planning on playing the song I wrote for the competition last, after a couple of jazz standards. So first we've got 'Giant Steps' and 'Take the "A" Train.'"

"That's great. That'll be just fine," he said, smiling. But then his expression changed. He pulled at one eyebrow and smiled crookedly. He looked a little shy, or maybe it was sly, Simone couldn't decide which; then he made a request. "Say, there are a few friends of mine here, jazz fans, and we play together a bit when we can. What do you say to moving 'Take the "A" Train' to the end of the list and letting us sit in with you? I promise we'll help you get a good score!"

Simone's mouth dropped open but no words came out. What could she say? The judge wanted to join her group! But what if they couldn't play together? What if Mr. Cantor and his friends were awful? He saw confusion taking over her face and added, "How about if your band plays through the whole song alone one time, and we'll join in for an encore. How would that be?"

Simone gave a sigh of relief, then answered, "That sounds fair. I'd like you to hear it the way we practiced it for the contest before adding more instruments." *Or before trying to play with a bunch of old guys we don't know, who probably know bluegrass instead of jazz,* she thought, keeping that

69
♪

comment to herself. She whispered the plan to the guys in her band and they echoed her doubts. But the deed was done. Mr. Cantor had gone to the mike to announce them.

He smiled widely, greatly satisfied with the arrangement, and introduced Blueberry Koffee to the crowd. "Okay, all right, now I'm just so happy you've all come 'round to hear this next group. Their name is Blueberry Koffee, but somebody made a mistake on your program, probably me. I am getting a little fuzzy in the ears at my age. I heard the name 'Blueberry' and thought 'bluegrass,' but, folks, this group may play blues more than bluegrass. Not tonight, though. Tonight they are playing straight up jazz for your enjoyment." Several older men in the front row, probably Mr. Cantor's musician friends (since they carried instrument cases), whistled and cheered while there was appreciative applause from the rest of the crowd. Maybe there really were jazz fans here. Maybe these older people had actually heard the great bands of Simone's grandparents' generation. If so, she hoped they were open to new arrangements, because her band's style would be a bit off the beaten path from jazz standard. Maybe she should have checked "Eclectic" on the entry under "Music Style," even though they played songs from the jazz book. Too late now. She'd have to live with "Jazz" as her description and so would the audience. She clicked the keys on her sax nervously, as if to make sure they were all still there, while Mr. Cantor finished talking. She didn't really hear another word he said until he waved his hand in her direction and said grandly, "Ladies and gentlemen, Blueberry Koffee will now serve up 'Giant Steps' for your enjoyment!"

Simone counted off for the band. Holding her sax in both hands, she stomped her right foot down behind her so they could all see her count each beat. "One, two, …" They all looked at her and then at each other. They were so ready. Simone flashed them a grin over her shoulder before she started playing.

"Giant Steps" by the great John Coltrane is a challenging piece and showed off all their technical skills individually and as a band. It was a great choice to introduce their band and let a judge know they could handle complex music. The guys played it as nearly perfect as anyone could expect. They added their own style, but didn't meddle too much with the masterpiece.

Surprise of surprises, the audience clapped loud and long at the end of "Giant Steps," and a few whistles and cheers came again from Mr. Cantor's musicians. *Wow, they loved it,* Simone thought. Mr. Cantor stood and motioned toward Simone, calling out, "Simone Leuw on saxophone, ladies and gentlemen." She bowed and then turned to her band and pointed to each of the guys in turn, shouting out their names. "Moby Dickinson on guitar. Greg Doyle on bass and his twin brother, Conan, on drums. And this is Adam Evans on bari sax." The crowd continued clapping and cheering at each name as if they had been starving to hear jazz.

Simone felt as if playing that piece well had earned her the right to ask the audience to give her own composition

71

a fair hearing. "Raindrops in Moonlight" was jazz music at the core, but she added a lot of melodic surprises of her own. She'd tried to write a piece of music that would express all her feelings of the last few months, the confusion about her strange talent for truth, the mystery of her mom's absence, the loneliness, the strange half-remembered dream, her drive to perfect her music—everything! Would this audience and the elderly judge be able to relate to it? She couldn't worry about that now. As soon as the clapping stopped, she counted the band in.

Simone played her heart out and the guys followed her every step of the way, supporting her every wish on a wave of sound. Tears formed in the corners of her eyes when she played the parts she had written to express her fears about her mom's secret. It was a difficult piece, almost as tough as "Giant Steps" in its own way. The audience knew it. When the song ended they broke out clapping just as they had for the first song.

Simone was shaken as much by the performance as by the audience appreciation. She hung her head for a few seconds, then turned and extended her arms as if to embrace the whole band in a hug. The crowd went wild. When they finished applauding, she spoke into the mike.

"Whew! Thank you so much, everyone. We really appreciate your warm welcome. Now it's time to have some fun. Get on board; we're going for a ride on the 'A' Train." The audience knew that title. They cheered. Simone continued, "I'd like to invite Mr. Cantor and company to join us on stage. I'll let him introduce his friends."

The judge stood and came up to the stage, followed by four grinning, silver-haired men carrying their music cases. "Well, you all know me as Ed Cantor, but some here can remember when I was known as 'Eddie the Earl' and I played this clarinet with these gentlemen as part of the band called 'Special Delivery.'" The crowd cheered. They remembered. "Here's 'Firebelly Floyd' Koehler on the sax, 'Smiles' Troxler on trumpet, 'Pistol Paul' Bissell on trombone. The days when we were a band and jazz was heard all over this town on the weekends were long ago, but we're going to see if we can still deliver something special for you tonight. Blueberry Koffee is going to start up the 'A' Train and they gave us tickets to get on at the station. So, Madame Conductor, start up those engines please, and let's get underway."

The elderly musicians took their places on stage and got their instruments out, and Simone motioned to her band. They began playing "Take the 'A' Train" with a long opening note that sounded like an old-fashioned train whistle.

The piece was just as challenging as the first two. She hated to ask the guys to play it through twice, but by the time they got to the part where the old gentlemen would join them, she was actually looking forward to doing it again. They'd heard Blueberry Koffee's arrangement once through, so she felt it should be pretty easy for them to join in. It wasn't just easy, though—it was as simple as breathing for them. The old guys still had great skills, some of the best musicianship she'd ever heard. It was

73
♪

obvious they knew how to take the "A" Train forward and backward. She and her band were the ones who had to work hard to keep up. By the time the song was ending, the crowd were on their feet clapping and dancing. Simone was almost out of breath after trading solos with spry old "Firebelly Floyd," who looked more like he should be sitting in a rocking chair than rocking the stage. Firebelly didn't appear stressed in the least, however.

"Thank you, sweetheart," he said demurely. She was glad he hadn't patted her on the head—she already felt like one of the scarecrow tap dancers compared with the old sax player and his skill that seemed to come so easily. Adam was completely impressed as well. He just mouthed the word "Wow!" as he caught his breath.

9

Confusions, Conclusions

WHACK! The end of a branch hit Billy Joe's visor as he swerved too late coming up the rough path through the woods. It wasn't big enough to do more than startle him, but he flinched and lost his balance. He planted his foot on the ground and slid the the green Honda motorcycle in a curve around it, stopping it on the pivot point. He adjusted his helmet and got ready to climb the next hill on his way home. It wasn't a great path, but it was a great shortcut he'd discovered thanks to Marti and Angela. He could see the cottage where the biggest adventure of his life had taken place. It looked so normal in the light of day. Just a little broken-down house that had been abandoned for years until the girls began poking around there and discovered its secret.

Billy Joe was about to rev his bike and zoom past the place when he saw something moving. It looked like someone was there. He kept his foot on the ground, balancing his bike, and lifted his bug-smeared visor. There was someone sitting on the sagging porch of the little cottage. Someone with spiky blond hair. Someone he really enjoyed seeing. It was Marti.

His heart gave a little hop, like a tiny lightning bolt had struck it. He wiped his visor off and fixed his helmet hair in the bike mirror. She hadn't seen him yet, but her black Arabian horse had obviously heard the bike and was looking in his direction. Billy Joe shut off his engine and pushed the bike down the hill. No sense in getting on her bad side by scaring her precious horse. He had something to ask her and didn't want to get a negative answer.

"Hi, Marti," he said as he leaned his bike on its kickstand. Then he almost jumped out of his skin when he saw a shadowy figure moving around behind her in the little cottage. He started to call out a warning, when the figure stepped out into the afternoon sunlight.

"You look like you've seen a ghost, Billy Joe," Angela joked, giggling a little as she came out the door.

"No, I didn't, I jus—" Billy Joe started to protest, but was startled again when another person suddenly stepped out the door just behind Angela.

"Hey, take it easy, guy," Kyle said. "No fallen angels here today. Just us chickens."

Billy Joe turned several shades of red in embarrassment. No sense in denying it. They had scared him. "Well, who wouldn't be jumping at shadows around here after what happened? It's not every day you see the kind of things we saw here."

"Yeah, we've stopped here a few times since then, but it seems like everything's returned to normal," Angela told him. "It's just a dusty old cabin again. Same for our barn and the school. I guess the good angel really did lock the door to all The Lines."

"It's okay by me. I'm not sure I want to see anything like that again. It makes me nervous to know there might be Angel Lines in other places, since your uncle saw one open up in Paris. I hope this place is locked for good," Kyle said.

"Yeah, I'm hoping not to see anything supernatural again," Angela agreed. "Well, maybe I'd be okay with the good angel. I don't think angels are beings you'd call up just to chat, but I think I'd like to see it again if I ever needed help."

Marti stood up and walked down the rickety porch stairs to Billy Joe. "I'm not so sure about that. The angel was very beautiful and it definitely rescued us all, but I like my heroes to look a little more . . . normal." She gave Billy Joe a dazzling smile to let him know the heroism he showed that day was still appreciated.

He wished Angela and Kyle would leave. He'd rather talk to Marti alone. How could he let them know four's a crowd? Before he had time to come up with a plan, they granted his wish.

77

"Don't mean to rush off, but we were just leaving when you showed up," Angela said. She hopped down from the porch and walked toward the back of the cottage, where her horse was nudging Kyle's minibike as if trying to knock it over. "Kyle is going to help me finish a project that's due tomorrow, so we have to go. We were just riding halfway home with Marti. Now that you're here, maybe you can go the rest of the way with her?"

"Sure, no problem. It's on my way," Billy Joe tried to answer casually, but his heart was thumping out of his chest. Now he had no excuse not to ask her the question that had been tormenting him all week. After much internal debate, he had definitely decided to ask her to be his date for the school dance—there was just no point in going unless it was with Marti.

Even though he was a senior in high school, he'd never bothered to go to a dance before. Why should he start now? The only reason was to take Marti somewhere special. Would she say yes? Would she say it before he had a heart attack? Not many guys his age had heart attacks, but he'd heard of some. Unexpectedly. Tragically. Probably caused by stress and undiagnosed congenital defects. Great—now he was sweating, and she was looking at him like she thought something was wrong. Could girls smell fear?

"Uh, okay, Angela. See you guys at school tomorrow," Marti said, as she turned to wave to her friends, still looking at Billy Joe out of the corner of her eye as if she thought he was going to do something weird. Then she asked, "So how are you going to go home with me? You can't ride that noisy bike next to Bobcat. He hates it."

"Let's just walk. That way we can talk. I'll push my bike," Billy Joe said, again trying to look casual (but probably just making his face look strangely uncomfortable). "We can take our time. It's not even close to dark."

So she led her horse and he pushed the motorcycle. "So what do you want to talk about?" she asked, focusing her beautiful hazel eyes on his face. Billy Joe was amazed at how extraordinary her eyes looked in the sunlight that filtered through the green leaves of the trees forming an arch over the narrow path. They almost made him dizzy, like when he stood on the edge of a lake and watched the waves and felt like the water was pulling him in.

"Your eyes," he said, and then realized he had nowhere to go with that. "Uh, your eyes are hazel, right?"

"Right."

"Uh, it must be the sunlight. They look more green than usual."

He notices my eyes? she wondered. Billy Joe was a mystery to her most of the time. Sometimes he acted like a boyfriend, and other times he seemed to go out of his way to make it clear he thought of her as just another friend. *It isn't as if I need him to be my boyfriend,* she thought. *I'm not looking for that.* But it seemed like he had been trying to get her to feel that way about him when he'd say something like the comment about her eyes— but he said things like that only about half the time. Confusing.

79

"Well, it just depends on what I'm wearing or what's around me. My eyes look greener when I'm around that color and more gray or brown when I'm not."

"Oh, oh, I see. Well, that makes sense." Awkward silence followed and Billy Joe panicked inside. *Think of something else to say. Something that will lead into talking about the dance. What could possibly lead into talking about dancing? Think. Music?*

"So, Chuck and I are learning some new music for Sunday service. It's, uh, new and all. Um, you and Angela have lots of friends who play music. Do you play an instrument?"

"Oh, no. I'm not musical, not me. I can't even sing."

They came to the place where the path connected to the main paved road. Hearing a car coming, they paused on the trail to let it pass by before crossing. The car slowed to a stop and several kids waved to them. The red-haired guy driving opened the window and called out, "Marti! Hey!" He waved her over to the car. She dropped Bobcat's reins and he stopped obediently where he was, so she approached the road without him. She talked to the guy in the car a minute, and it seemed as if he was asking her something, because she nodded and seemed to agree. She waved to him and his friends, and then returned to Billy Joe and her horse as the car drove away.

"That was Rick," she said as if the statement explained everything. It didn't. Not to Billy Joe's satisfaction. But he'd learned that Marti and Angela had the impression he was sometimes bossy, and he really wanted to change that image. So he didn't ask. He tried to get back to the subject he'd started. They were almost to her house, so he was running out of time.

"So, I like all kinds of music, not just the kind Chuck and I play at church," he said. "I heard there's going to be a pretty good band at that dance they're having at school after break."

"Oh, really?" Marti said.

Not much for him to work with. "Uh, yeah, that's what they say. I'm kind of interested in hearing them." He waited three beats. Four beats. *She isn't going to say anything back. Try again.* "I mean, it sounds like it could be fun. Are you planning on going?"

"I hadn't really thought about it," she answered. It was true. Marti wasn't sure why Billy Joe was acting so uncomfortable, but she didn't guess what was on his mind.

"Well, I've been thinking about it. What I've been thinking is that it might be fun to go together. I actually haven't dated much, but Marti, I think you are a very special girl. You're different from other girls. I feel like you are my friend, and I like being friends with you. I just think we might be more than friends."

Now she stopped walking and stared at him. She took a breath like she was about to talk, but she still didn't say anything. It was agonizing for him to stand there as she stared at him. Impossible to read her expression.

Maybe he hadn't been clear. He tried again. "What I'm trying to do is ask you to go on a date with me. A date to the school dance. What do you think?"

81

Marti thought so many things about that subject it was impossible for her to put them into words quickly. "Well, this is kind of complicated. Can I call you later?"

That was not the response he expected. He looked down at the ground to avoid her eyes as he tried to recover his train of thought. That was when he noticed the silver ring on her left hand. It had a heart with a small diamond in the middle. What did that mean? Did it have something to do with that guy in the car—that Rick guy?

Marti noticed Billy Joe staring at her new ring. Now that it came to the moment she and her parents had talked about, Marti couldn't decide exactly what to say about the ring. She decided to wait and see if Billy Joe asked her anything—it might be easier if she could just answer questions about it.

He didn't ask her anything, but he should have.

Billy Joe let his mind race to a conclusion that kept him from talking to her any more about the dance. He wasn't in any of Marti's classes. She might have a serious relationship with someone else already, and he realized he hadn't yet given her any reason to report that to him. Fine. He was too late. His heart thudded, like it had turned to molten rock and dropped to the bottom of a well. Love hurt.

Marti was unaware any of this was going on in his head. They both had too much to say and no way to say it. Billy Joe looked at Marti and she seemed to be all blurry. His thoughts were dizzying.

Marti's thoughts were like alphabet soup with no letters forming into words. She wanted to tell him all about the conversation she'd had with her parents after their last counseling session. It seemed like a miracle that she and Angela had been talking about dating at the same time her parents had been discussing it with Pastor James. When they went home, her folks talked to her, and then they all prayed together in such a sincere way, a deep spiritual feeling grew between them that their family never had felt together before. That weekend, she and her dad picked out the silver ring together at a jewelry store, and tears filled her eyes when he put it on her finger. But she wasn't sure how to explain all this to Billy Joe.

She needed help and her dad had promised to help her about this kind of thing. It all sounded so easy when they discussed it, but now that she had to tell Billy Joe about it, she was speechless. Dad would know what she could say to Billy Joe.

"I'll call you," she said when she saw her house ahead. She touched his shoulder briefly before she leapt up into Bobcat's saddle.

Billy Joe had a lump in his throat that felt as if he'd swallowed a golf ball. He just nodded and put his motorcycle helmet over his head, looking away as Marti rode off.

Angela and Kyle rode back to her place, horse and motorcycle going along on the path together. Kyle's bike was more a scooter than a motorcycle, so even Marti's

83

horse wasn't scared of it as long as he didn't start it up without any warning. Angela's mustang, Roy Rogers, was bold enough to canter right alongside the scooter without a worry. Sara Grace called Roy "bomb-proof" in traffic noise, even though he was cautious about new noises he'd never heard. The key was that once he found out that something didn't scare Angela, it didn't scare him.

Nothing about Kyle scared Angela. They had been friends since elementary school, though they had started out as competitors; Kyle always won the spelling bees for the boys' side and Angela was usually the champ for the girls' side. Gradually those lines blurred and their group of friends included both sexes. The Barn fellowship where Angela's family belonged was a lot like the evangelical church where Kyle's parents were youth leaders. Angela envied Kyle because he had always embraced his parents' beliefs and never seemed to doubt the Bible teaching he heard in Sunday school. But that was Kyle: Once he researched something and formed an opinion about it, he wasn't easily swayed.

When they pulled up at Angela's house, she untacked her horse. Kyle offered to help, and carried the saddle to its rack in the "secret room" they used for storage at the back of the barn. He glanced at the ancient sketches of stars and stick figures carved onto the stones at the base of the wall, then looked around the place, remembering what had happened there just a couple of weeks ago. Except for the drawings, the room was unremarkable and seemed to have returned to normal, just as the cabin in the woods had done. No more angels or strange lights. It was hard to believe anything out of the ordinary had happened there. Kyle shrugged and pulled the door shut.

Angela's horse reached over the half-door of his stall and nudged Kyle's shoulder with his nose in a chummy way. "Roy's not jealous of you, like he is of some people," Angela said, smiling. "He actually shoves in between me and my dad if we're talking and not paying any attention to him."

Kyle tipped his head and grinned the way he did when he had a secret to tell. "I think he likes me, and he knows he can count on a couple of these." He pulled a roll of mints from his pocket. Roy nodded his head like a trick pony and Kyle slipped him a candy.

"So that's your secret! You've been bribing my horse with sugar!" She grabbed a wisp of hay and tried to stuff it in the neck of Kyle's shirt. "You're turning my horse into a junk food addict."

Kyle ducked and spun out of her reach. Roy turned his back on them, savoring the forbidden treat, with his head in the far corner of his stall to make sure Angela couldn't fish it out of his mouth. For the moment, she had turned all her attention on Kyle, determined he should pay for his crime, but he was fast and grabbed a handful of the prickly hay to defend himself.

"En garde!" he called out and flourished the strands like a rubbery sword.

"Yeah, right!" Angela jumped up on a nearby bale of straw and was suddenly a foot taller than he. She stuffed

85

the hay down his collar while keeping her bare neck out of reach. They each managed to get plenty of the scratchy stuff in their clothes before it was over, and both began yelling "Ouch!" and "Truce!"

"Stop or I'm telling your mom," Kyle threatened. That was what he used to say when they were little kids. Angela remembered and laughed.

"I'm telling my dad," she countered. Kyle got the point.

"Okay, you win." He dropped his fistfuls of hay and held up empty hands, then becoming serious, he said: "But maybe there is something I should tell your dad. Should I tell him about the dance?"

"I already did," Angela said.

"And?"

"No problem. I explained it wasn't a date."

"Oh, good . . . unless you think it should be."

"Should be what?"

"A date." Kyle brushed the hay off his coat and picked a strand out of Angela's hair. "I've been thinking about all this. We've known each other a long time, and we're used to doing things together as friends. But I don't want to be dishonest with the one person I can always tell everything to."

"And if you were going to tell me everything, you'd say . . . what?" Angela asked.

Kyle leaned closer and she could smell the mint on his breath. "I'd say of all the girls I know anywhere, you are the only one I'd consider a serious relationship with."

Angela knew those words meant the same thing to Kyle as they did to her. Kyle and his parents had been at the same dating seminar she had gone to with her folks. They both knew the rules and knew they'd promised to involve their parents in any such decision.

"Thanks," she said, out of breath, but not from the hay fight. Her heart was doing some kind of funny fluttery thing she'd never really felt around Kyle before.

10

The Next Stop

M R. CANTOR'S WIFE did not look at all like him—
he was tall and square-shouldered, she was
shorter and round everywhere, including her
soft hairdo that sat on her head like a cotton ball hat. But
the couple seemed to look very much alike in one
sense—they had identical satisfied smiles. When Mrs.
Cantor smiled it was not smug or stuck on herself, but at
peace with who she was—so much so her inner peace
seemed to reach out to embrace everyone else and make
them feel the same way when she was around. When
Moby met her, he thought, *There's a lady who is comfortable in her own skin.*

Her house seemed as if it were smiling, too. Velvety
African violets of every color peeked out of tiny pots on
windowsills and corner tables. Two playful calico kittens

hopped up and down on an overstuffed couch in the living room. She served her guests warm cocoa and cookies on lacquered trays, her gentle laugh and smile crinkles at the corners of her eyes welcoming them. After the group became sleepy from the cushioned furniture and warm drink, she opened the door to a long guest room at the back of her house, and the boys saw she had made up four cots along the outer wall, under a bank of windows that overlooked a moonlit garden. At the far end of the room was the door to a big, tiled shower room with stacks of fluffy towels waiting in a basket by the entrance.

"Now, you boys make yourselves at home here. If you get hungry, go in the kitchen and help yourselves. If there's anything you need, just ask. Mr. Cantor will be down here in his study for a while yet tonight."

Turning to Simone, she took the girl's hand and patted it. "Come with me, sweetheart. I made up my daughter Emily's old room for you to use."

At the top of a carpeted staircase, Mrs. Cantor switched on the light in a room just above the one the boys were using. Simone gasped when she saw the darling place. In one corner, a yellow, flowered quilt covered a white wicker bed filled with plump pillows. A carved rocking horse that looked like a real antique waited in another corner next to a wicker dresser and a matching shelf of knickknacks and small books. There was a white wicker rocker under a curtained window in the other corner. As Simone was staring, her hostess opened a door

89

next to the rocker and said, "The bathroom is in here and I've laid out some towels for you."

Simone looked inside and gasped again when she saw the big old-fashioned bathtub with a thick white rug next to it, a basket of colorful soaps, a bottle of pink bubble bath, and an array of candles. Before she knew it, Mrs. Cantor had left her alone and she was sitting in the tub with sparkling bubbles up to her chin and three vanilla-scented candles glowing in the background. The music of the day wove in and out of her thoughts as she enjoyed her reward, especially sweet after all the hard work it had taken to get there. She couldn't imagine any rock star getting better treatment anywhere than she was enjoying at this wonderful, peaceful place.

"Thank you, God. It's so much better than anything I could have imagined to ask for myself," she prayed, smiling and sliding down in the scented water.

The morning at Mr. and Mrs. Cantor's house was just as sweet as the night had been. All the dark thoughts she'd been hoarding about what she'd say when Doug Wembly phoned with instructions about their next gig were drowned in homemade maple syrup as she munched on golden pancakes at the Cantors' breakfast table.

"All's well that ends well," Mr. Cantor quoted Shakespeare as he poured coffee for everyone and winked. "I got to play with some promising new jazz talent and the crowd loved it just as much as they would have loved bluegrass music. Sorry you had to put up with a group of geriatrics, but maybe you'll get an audience more your own age at the next place. It sounds like a college gig."

"Hey, Mr. C. We had a great time playing with your band," Moby said sincerely. "I bet I learned more in one night of playing with you guys than a whole semester at a music school."

"Yeah, it's a crime you aren't teaching technique at a college somewhere," Greg agreed.

"Oho! That would be the wrong venue for us," Mr. Cantor said, raising one hand as if the thought were too much. "We're free spirits, not syllabus types. We could never put all we know down on paper. You just have to be there to learn it from us. And only certain students would understand what that is—you guys are unique. Not every musician, young or old, would get us."

"Well, we were lucky to 'be there' at the right time," Conan said, nodding as if the music were still playing in his head.

"Yep, it was one of those things. Those things that keep you alive and looking for the next thing," Mr. Cantor said dreamily.

Wembly still hadn't called Simone as promised and she only got his voice mail when she tried to call him. "We have general directions," she said. "Let's get on the road and I'll try calling him as we drive."

"Hey, Mr. Cantor, I can't get on your wireless, can you reset the router?" Greg asked, trying to download a map on his laptop.

"I have no idea what you just said, but if you're trying to get on the Internet with that, you'll have to go to the café uptown or stop at the library. My old computer isn't hooked up to anything but the electric outlet in the wall," the old gentleman said.

"Eddie, it's too early for the library to be open yet. Just give them a real map," Mrs. Cantor said, scolding him and bringing out a folded map from a kitchen drawer.

"Yes, take this, kids. It's not flashy, but it'll get you where you want to go." Mr. Cantor's chair creaked across the tiles as he took the well-worn map from his wife and handed it to Greg.

They piled their belongings back into the SUV and started out with full stomachs and hopeful hearts that day. They figured they would probably stay full from the generous breakfast until after lunch, and they planned to stop for early dinner near Oxford, where Adam's older brother lived on a small farm with his wife and baby. There wasn't any point in getting to their next gig too early, and they didn't want to eat dinner too close to performing.

"Hi, Ben. We're on our way. Yes. Sure, I bet they'll love it. Thanks. See you then." Adam hung up. "His wife won't be home, but he wants to take us out to his country club to eat."

"You're kidding," Greg said. "He wants to 'eat at the club'? He must be rich."

"No, not rich—he's a middle school teacher and he loves to golf, so they joined this unusual golf club. It's

called The Mounds and it's built on some kind of archaeological site. Don't get too excited that it's called a country club. I don't think it's all that posh, but it sounds
interesting and worth a stop. I mean, we have to get dinner somewhere. My brother hasn't been back home in
months, so it'll be great to see him again."

"Hey, man, it's sure to be more posh than a truck
stop. And it sounds like your bro is buying," Moby said
contentedly.

"And we can get out of the car to eat," Simone said.
They'd aired out the SUV overnight and she didn't want
any more fast food funk to invade the vehicle.

The Mounds Country Club looked like a huge
lodge made of logs and stone, with colorful geometric
artwork everywhere. The simple figures reminded Simone
of Egyptian hieroglyphics, but she didn't know enough
about that to decide what they were.

Adam's brother was waiting for them just inside the
door and started waving when he saw them getting out
of the car. He looked like a slightly older version of
Adam, a little more muscled with a dark beard stubble
that Adam didn't have yet. She couldn't help thinking,
This is what Adam will look like when he is in his twenties.

"Adam! Oh, man! It's good to see you!" Ben said,
grabbing his younger brother in a big hug, so the two big
guys looked like a couple of bears beginning a wrestling
match.

"This must be your band. Welcome, welcome. I've
heard good things about you. I'm Benjamin, you must

93

have guessed. You must be Simone." Clearly, Ben was the talkative extrovert brother. Simone introduced herself and the band as soon as Ben released her hand from an enthusiastic shaking.

"Come on in. I've got a table over there, but you can follow me through the buffet line first." They followed Ben's lead, filling plates with fried catfish, hamburgers, barbequed chicken, sweet potatoes, and other substantial food. The Mounds chef obviously favored hearty homestyle foods over fancy meals. The band approved.

"Now that's a great buffet," Conan said between bites.

"I'm guessing you eat here a lot, bro," Adam said, poking Ben in the belly.

"It catches up with you," Ben admitted. "And they have a choice of three kinds of pie for dessert."

Simone swallowed her third bite of delicious catfish and pointed to a primitive mural on the wall near them. It looked like a female figure leading several males in a footrace. "What's that artwork about?"

"That is the story of an Indian princess who didn't want to take a husband," Ben told her. "See how she's racing ahead of the young braves following her? Her father commanded that she marry the brave who could defeat her in a race. She knew that whoever she married would rule the tribe instead of her, so she filled her apron with apples and threw them at the head of each brave as he got close to her. She knocked each one down as he came near, and won the race, so she became the matriarch of her tribe."

Conan pointed at the artwork with his thumb and leaned toward the other guys. "Hm-m-m, the anti-Sleeping Beauty, I guess."

"I like her," Simone said with a smirk. "So what tribe made this art?"

"There's a little question about that," Ben explained. "Some think it was the Hopewell Indians because they are so old, beyond the recorded history of any tribe that exists today. Other researchers think a group of explorers from Asia came here across a land bridge or something, because that story and others they've found are similar to Greek and Egyptian myths. They also think some of the artifacts found here look more Egyptian style than Native American style. Then, of course, there are the pyramids . . ."

"What pyramids?" Simone wanted to know.

"This golf course is built around a 50-acre circle of six mounds that European settlers thought looked like pyramids with the tops cut off. If you want to see them, we can take a quick walk to work off lunch when we're finished."

"Wait, are you saying there are Egyptian pyramids in Ohio?" Moby asked.

Ben shook his head. "I'm not saying anything, except that it's an interesting archaeological mystery. Maybe it was just a coincidence these Native Americans built mounds that look like pyramids. This is a fertile farming and game area. The first people who lived here might have had an easier life than tribes who lived in harsher places. Maybe they had more time for art and imagination, so they happened on the pyramid idea creatively. They were a very ancient people, and their culture vanished long ago, so all we can do is guess. The mounds aren't burial chambers like the Egyptian pyramids. They might have been built for religious ceremonies, or defense positions against invading tribes, or as raised places to live on safe from floods. No one knows for sure. I'll show them to you and you can judge for yourself."

Simone could picture Ben giving this lecture to his middle school class. She guessed he was one of those teachers students loved to get assigned to—they'd learn all the required information without feeling as if they were being taught. She imagined he took his classes on field trips and played games to review for tests.

After the guys plundered the pie selection at the buffet, they were so full of heavy food that Ben's suggestion of a short walk seemed essential before riding in the car again. They were only a half-hour drive from their venue, so they still had an hour before they'd need to leave. They walked the golf cart path behind a group of four jolly retirees who invited them to come along and watch them play. The fall colors were waning as sunset approached, but the air was still warm. With the evergreen trees and the tended grass on the course still green, it felt more like a late summer afternoon than winter.

The first pyramid was at the end of the second hole. The course had been designed to weave in and out of the circle of hills, rather than go over them. The elevation increased as they reached the first of the circle of mounds, and they were soon unbuttoning their coats, heating up from the exercise.

"I'm wishing we had golf carts ourselves right now," Greg said as he watched the golfers speed their carts up the hill to the putting green ahead of them.

"That's the first pyramid," Ben said pointing to a grassy hill behind the green, where the golfers were getting ready to putt.

"It does look like a pyramid with the top cut off," Moby said, shielding his eyes with one hand and squinting at the hill.

"Are there blocks of stone underneath that look like the pyramids in Egypt?" Conan asked.

"No, it's just rocks, gravel, and dirt piled up under the sod. They're full of artifacts like arrowheads, copper jewelry, and small, stone hand tools," Ben replied. His cell phone rang and he stopped to answer. "What? Is that you, honey? I can't hear you . . . I'm on the course. Call you back." He clicked his phone shut and pointed to a metal tower. "Cell phones won't work on the course. Even with that new tower up there."

"Cell phones won't work here?" Adam frowned and looked at the landscape. "That's weird. It's all open field from here to the tower. You should have great reception."

"Yeah, they've sent crews out several times to troubleshoot it, but no luck." Ben tucked his phone back in his pocket as the golfers drove by, finished with that hole.

"You can't call anyone out here," one of the old guys yelled when he saw Ben putting his phone away.

97
♪

"Yeah, and nobody can call you while you're golfin', either. It makes my wife so mad," said one of the others with a big laugh.

"It's them witchin' stones," the oldest-looking man of the group said solemnly.

That got Moby's attention. "What's a witching stone?"

"Oh, shut up, Barley, don't go scarin' the kids with your ghost stories," the golfer steering the cart told his buddy.

"Ha! It's no story. I'll show you." The wizened old man climbed down from his seat and pulled a shiny putter from his worn leather golf bag. "Now, you all watch this. I'll prove it to you, Jerry."

Barley walked over to the edge of the mound, and held the grip of the club in one hand, letting the club hang loosely, pointing down to the ground. Slowly, the club began swinging slightly. "I'm not making it do that," Barley said seriously. He turned and looked at the group with a somewhat scared expression. "I swear. It's those black stones in the mound. They're like magnets."

Jerry grabbed the putter and shooed his friend back to the cart. "Bah! C'mon, stop that. You're holding up the game. Next thing you'll want to try finding water with that club—or fairies!"

Adam chuckled and turned to see what Simone thought of the old man's story. She looked at him strangely, glassy-eyed, then sunk slowly to the ground in a heap.

11

One Small Step

SIMONE WATCHED Barley's golf club swing once, twice, and then as it began a third arc, it looked like the putter was cutting into a patch of fog. It was strange in the bright afternoon sun to see fog. She looked at Adam to ask if he saw it, and that was when she noticed everyone around her had become clouded, blurry, as if the fog had suddenly sprung up from the ground under the course to enclose everything. The ground underfoot felt like it was turning into Jell-O, and her companions had startled looks on their faces as they watched her fall to her knees and close her eyes.

When she opened her eyes again, the people who had been there were gone. The sunshine was gone. The pyramid was the only familiar thing left, but it had changed. The grassy hill had been transformed to a glass wall and there was now a triangular top to the pyramid, shiny and pointing to a darkening sky. She sat up and looked around. She could see human silhouettes moving near the other side of the pyramid. Was it Adam and the guys? She tried to call out, but she couldn't hear her own voice make a sound, though she felt as if she was screaming. The people over there didn't seem to see or hear her, but she could hear them talking, their voices muffled over the distance. They were moving away from her. She tried yelling again. As they walked closer to the glass wall, light coming from inside the structure illuminated them. Three of the people she didn't recognize, but the fourth was definitely familiar. It was her mom.

At that moment, her mom turned and looked her way, then called out, "Simone!" She put out her hand and took a step toward Simone. Suddenly, the ground began to shake and Simone struggled to balance herself on hands and knees to keep from falling. The shaking increased in the ground underneath her and it seemed to make everything around her blur. She heard a voice next to her.

"Simone! Hey, are you okay?"

She felt the ground become solid again. As the person came into focus and the world stopped shaking, she saw it wasn't her mom saying her name, but Adam's brother. "Ben, what are you doing here?" she whispered.

"What am I doing here? Where else would I be? Where were *you*?" he asked.

"I think I was in Paris," she said, looking up into his frightened face.

Ben offered her a bottle of water. "You fainted, Simone. Drink this. Maybe you got dehydration from all your traveling and excitement."

Simone drank some water, but she wasn't very thirsty. They'd just had a big dinner and plenty of water. She knew what she'd seen wasn't a hallucination. The whole experience had the ring of truth.

Now the truth was unclear—where was she? Not on the golf course. She sat up and looked around. It was a hospital room.

"How did . . . where am I?"

"This is Oxford Medical Center," Ben told her. "We brought you here when we couldn't revive you. Lucky for you there are always plenty of doctors sitting around the clubhouse lounge. There were actually three doctors wasting time there when you passed out, but I picked this one because he looked like he'd work cheap." Adam's brother pointed to a man about his own age wearing a collared golf shirt with a stethoscope hung around his neck.

"Ha, ha! Very funny coming from a guy who still owes me for delivering his baby," the man said poking a finger in Ben's chest. "He also has no manners, a product of public education, so I'll introduce myself. I'm Dr. Gatewood. Can you tell me what happened?"

Simone didn't know exactly what to say to a stranger about what had happened. If she told a doctor everything she and her friends had experienced with the supernatural lately, he'd probably lock her up in a padded cell. She decided to tell him just the symptoms a doctor could understand.

"I felt dizzy and I fell to the ground. I guess I passed out, because everyone disappeared for a minute."

Dr. Gatewood did the usual doctor things: took her pulse, looked at her eyes with a flashlight, and asked if she had any food allergies. "Did you get stung by a bee or anything out there? Are you allergic to bee stings?"

"I didn't notice any bees. I'm not allergic to anything that I know of."

"Think you can stand up? Okay, let's see how your balance is." Simone got out of the bed and took a couple of steps. He asked her to raise her arms once.

"How do you feel? Any more dizziness?"

102

"No, I'm just tired. Like I've been running."

"Hm-m-m. Well, I shouldn't ignore that. I'll run a few more tests. Your dad is driving down here to pick you up, so we should be able to tell you both what happened by the time he gets here."

"My dad? Oh, no, that's not necessary. I'm sure I'm fine, Doctor. Thanks for your help. We really have to leave now or we'll be late for our performance."

Ben looked worried and uncomfortable. "You don't know if you're fine yet, Simone," he said frowning. "Your dad wants you to wait for him here and let the doctors check you out."

Simone looked around. The room was empty except for Ben and the doctor. That was wrong. "How long was I unconscious? Where's Adam? Where are the guys?"

"Well, they wanted to just stay here and skip the whole thing, but when they couldn't get in touch with anyone by phone, they decided to drive over and find whoever is in charge to cancel in person."

"Cancel! No, no, no, we can't cancel!" Simone fell back onto the bed and put her face in her hands. How could it end like this? "Where's my phone?"

The doctor handed her purse over and she dug through it. Her phone was flashing. Two voice mails. The first was her dad. In no uncertain terms, he commanded her to wait right where she was for him to arrive. "Oh, Dad, don't you get it?" she muttered, deleting the message.

The next message was Adam. "Simone, we just got here. You are not going to believe it. College Corner is a town, not a venue, and it's not even in Ohio. We had to cross the border into Indiana. The address they sent us to is a high school. We're supposed to play at a high school dance—obviously, they're not going to want jazz. I don't know what we can do. Maybe improvise some pop stuff—we've all played in pep band . . . Man! Anyway, their school band director is a nice guy and the one who's supposed to judge us. Hopefully, we can help him out and stay in the competition. I swear I'm going to kill that Wembly guy. Anyway, if you're hearing this, you must be better. I hope you are. I, uh, I'll see you as soon as we get done here. Bye."

Simone looked at the time on the phone. The message was an hour old. What she'd seen in Paris had only taken seconds. How could she have been out cold for more than an hour?

Ben waited until she was done hearing Adam's message. "Did you hear Adam's message? I talked to him just before you woke up. The guys decided to try and play some music to help out the school band director. Adam said he seemed like a nice guy and was really grateful for any music they could get so their school dance wouldn't be ruined."

Simone laid her head back into the pillow and rolled her eyes. "I give up. This must be the craziest tour any band has ever had. That agent from the contest is out of his mind. He hasn't told us or anyone else the truth about anything since day one. The really crazy thing is, I knew he was lying about something—I just chalked it up to him being a slick PR guy who tells people what they want to hear. I had no idea he was lying about so many things. I guess I have a lot to learn about what's true and what's almost true."

"That's an interesting way to put it," Ben said. He tilted his head and seemed to be considering her words, looking at her as if she'd surprised him with a new idea. "I have to think about that. Maybe that's how deceivers work, they make statements that are 'almost true' and if we want to believe them, we can accept it as truth.

You know, the first lie the serpent told Eve in the Garden of Eden was like that, now that I think of it. He told her the forbidden fruit would make her the same as God because she'd know good from evil. It was almost true, because she did find out the difference between good and evil, but she and her husband became more like the opposite of God than like him."

"So the serpent took part of the truth and used it to lead Eve into a lie?"

"Maybe that's how it worked. Really sneaky, huh?" Ben said frowning. "I hear half-true arguments put out there to lead my middle school kids down the wrong path all the time. 'It's okay to cheat on a test if I don't get caught,' or 'If you're in love, sex without marriage is okay,' or 'It's okay to steal from a big department store. They're rich.' I guess kids want to believe things that will allow them to do what they want. Maybe this PR guy gets away with his lies because aspiring musicians want to believe him so badly. He probably believes telling people what they want to hear isn't actually lying."

Simone nodded. "Then every time he gets away with it, he gets rewarded for finding free talent, but the musicians are left holding a bag full of hot air. Like us."

"Well, it's not over yet. God can take the bad things that people try to do to us and turn them around for our good."

Ben sounded just like her dad. He must have been able to read her expression, because he hurried to add, "I'm starting to sound like my dad. But the older I get, the more I realize that the things our dad taught us from the Bible are true. I sure gave the old man a hard time about it when I was your age. I had to prove it to myself after I went off to college, but now I know. Adam and I

105
♪

were lucky to have been brought up by parents with faith."

Simone agreed, but she had her own concerns. "Well, yes, but don't you think people can take that idea of trusting God to take care of things too far? Isn't there a lot we need to do on our own to make sure things turn out okay?"

Ben rubbed the stubble on his cheek and almost looked like he was trying to keep from smiling. "I'm not so sure I'd say 'a lot.' But yes, you can't just pray you'll pass a test and not study. And sometimes we get ourselves into a tough spot because we make decisions without being able to know how everything will go ahead of time. But, Simone, I think the concept of making things turn out right is usually flawed. We want things to go the way we imagine is the right way. God sometimes has a different plan and a different idea of what 'turning out okay' means."

This did not seem helpful to Simone. She threw up her hands. "Well, you can't know everything ahead of time. And how can you find out what God's plan is for things that aren't written out in the Bible?"

Ben smiled. "That's what faith is all about. You read the Bible and you'll get to trusting the Author of it to finish the story in your life. That's also what prayer is for. If you want to pray about this whole situation, I think this would be a good time to do it. And prayer is never the wrong decision."

12

Face the Music

D A-A-AD!" Marti hollered as she slammed the front door. "Where are you?"

"I'm in here," her dad called from the kitchen. "Cheese sandwich?" he asked, holding up a long orange box of processed cheese food as Marti came sliding around the corner. "Ugh! No, thanks," she said making a rather rude gagging sound at the sight of the box. Dad had the worst taste in cheese, and he loaded his sandwiches with two-inch slabs of the fake orange stuff smothered in margarine. "I'm not in the mood for a grease sandwich right now."

"Your loss. This is great cheese. It never has any lumps like that deli stuff you and your mom like."

"Dad, I need to talk about something serious. It's about what we talked about Saturday."

Dad looked down, suddenly very busy with his sandwich preparation. "Really? Uh, well, good. You mean about dating? What's on your mind about it?" Then his face lit up like he had an inspiration. "Should I call your mom down here for this?"

"No, at least not yet. I have to ask you some things. I need a guy's point of view."

"Oh, well, I *used* to be a guy . . ." He rubbed his balding forehead and smirked. "When I was younger."

"Don't joke. I mean it. I need your help and you promised I can tell you anything and you won't go crazy about it." She sat down on a chair at the table across from him and folded her arms.

Dad straightened his shirt and sat down. This was it. He had run the scenario through his head a dozen times since meeting with Pastor James. There seemed to be a few options about how this could go, and all of them were uncharted waters for him. "Okay. All right. Tell me what I can do for you."

"I have a friend who is a guy. Not a boyfriend. Not yet. But he's asked me to go on a date with him. Officially." There, she'd said it. Marti saw her dad squirm in his seat, but she didn't know he was fighting the urge to yell, "No way! Go to your room!" He privately got control of himself.

"I see," he answered calmly. "Well, Marti, thank you so much for trusting me with this information and allowing

108

me to be part of your decision." *Did that sound rehearsed?* He hoped not, but the words felt stiff and not like his own. He'd try something more conversational. "How do you feel about this guy and your relationship with him?"

"Oh, Dad, I don't know. I really admire him in some ways. In other ways, I'm not so sure. He can be annoying. I don't know if he's someone I'd want to spend the rest of my life with yet. Do I have to know that before we go on a date?"

"No, I think that's taking the rules too far. You just want to remember what your goals are in life as a Christian and make sure any boy you build a relationship with has the same goals. Um, maybe you should tell me who this boy is and then I could give you some more specific advice." He felt pretty sure he knew who it was. He cringed.

"Well, it's Billy Joe Countryman," Marti said with a smile.

He knew it! He put the sandwich back on his plate carefully. Somehow he'd made rather deep finger imprints in the bread. Okay, he and Marti's mom had had a talk with Pastor James about the boy. Supposedly, Billy Joe was a believer who was in good standing in their church group. The pastor assured them he'd had many conversations with Billy Joe about how to treat girls with respect and how to honor their parents' authority. Fine. They'd have to put that to the test.

"Marti, have you and Billy Joe had a talk about the life goals we discussed?"

109
♪

"I didn't know how to bring it up. That's a pretty serious discussion."

"Well, dating is a serious thing to do. Why don't I invite Billy Joe over here, and we can help you have that talk with him?"

Marti looked at her father as if he had just told her he had six toes on one foot. She could certainly see how great he would be on her side in all this. He was calm and logical—that was part of his talent in the business world. He had a hidden talent—like a superhero or something—that he wanted to use on her behalf. "Dad, I think that would really help me. But you have to promise to not say anything embarrassing or make jokes about this. And you can't be too serious and make Billy Joe feel like he's getting interrogated, okay? And I think I should be the one to invite him. He might think something's wrong if you just call him up out of the blue."

110
♪

Angela and Kyle found her dad sitting in his favorite rocker in the kitchen, where he'd started a hearty fire in the huge, stone fireplace. He gently shook a long-handled popcorn popper over the flames, just close enough to start the kernels and oil whistling without burning them. Mom was pouring two mugs of apple cider and paused when she saw her daughter and Kyle. "Cider?"

"Yes, please," they both answered.

They took the mugs Mom offered and pulled up chairs by the fireplace. *Well, there will never be a better time than this,* Angela thought, and she nodded at Kyle. He suddenly felt really thirsty and buried his face in the mug of chilled cider. Coming up for air, he saw Angela frown a bit. All right. He didn't want to stutter or anything. Time to man up.

"You know, Mr. Clarkson, I really like . . ." *Too abrupt. Ease into it.* " . . . popcorn. I mean I like the kind you make with a real popper over the fire. That microwave stuff isn't as good. It's less crunchy."

"And less fun," Mr. Clarkson agreed. "Though you aren't as likely to burn the other kind or burn your fingers making it."

"Well, I've burnt both kinds," Kyle admitted, and then he had an idea. "That's why it's important to get advice from people who know what they're doing, like you and Mrs. Clarkson. You two have been making popcorn for years. You probably have all sorts of good advice about that . . . and lots of things."

"Well, we've been married for a long time. We've learned a lot along the way."

"I bet. So how did you meet?" Kyle looked over at Angela. Yep, she thought the conversation was headed in the right direction.

"At a barn, of course," Angela's mom answered. "Noel was our new blacksmith, fresh out of college. All the girls with horses found reasons to call him out there whenever they could."

"But you were the only one I called up," Mr. Clarkson said with a wink. Suddenly he turned to Kyle and gave him a long look. Maybe he was sitting too close

111

to the fire or something, because his face grew red. The popcorn started popping in the basket like tiny fireworks going off.

Angela's mom had been paying attention to all this. She warned her husband, "Keep shaking the popper, honey, or it will burn." Mr. Clarkson scooted the rocker around to face the fire and started shaking the popcorn popper more vigorously. He threw his wife a glance over his shoulder. She nodded.

"I think it's about time, dear. Here, let me put that in a bowl," she said, taking the long wooden handle away from her husband and carrying the popper to a large bowl on the kitchen counter. "Yes, this is the perfect moment." She nodded again and her husband got the signal. They had a plan and the moment had come to execute it.

Mr. Clarkson turned his seat back around, so he faced Kyle. "There's nothing like a good fire," he said. "It's a wonderful thing to have on a cold day; it can warm you up and cook your food. As long as it's in its proper place, it's a blessing."

Kyle nodded. Angela smiled. Mr. Clarkson unbuttoned his sweater and went on. "There are a lot of things in life like this fire. They are forces for good when they're used properly, but can be destructive if you don't use them the right way. A fire belongs in the fireplace." He leaned forward and gave Kyle eye contact that was meant to emphasize the unspoken point about fire.

"Oh, I agree," Kyle said, nodding a little too vigorously. "You can't play around with fire. Or things like that. You have to know what you're getting into . . . uh, this is kind of like something I want to talk to you about. Angela said she told you I asked her to go to the school dance with me, and I just want to let you know I understand the responsibility that goes along with that. I've been talking to my parents about it. We had a lot of good discussions after the conference last summer."

Angela's dad looked relieved. "Good. That was a great conference. I'd say I agree with everything they said there about the difference between the kind of casual dating you see on TV shows and the kind of relationship-building that pleases God. And you're right, it's a lot like this fire. Some kids play around with dating like kids running around with flaming sticks at a campfire. That's the way to get burnt. You have to begin with your life goals in mind."

"I get the feeling you and Kyle have a lot in common, including seeking God's goals for your lives," Mrs. Clarkson said to Angela.

"It's kind of amazing," Angela admitted. "We're very different in a lot of ways, but in the things that are really important, we agree. Know what I mean?"

Her mom nodded and smiled at her husband. She felt very pleased with her daughter's choice and with the sincere young man their neighbor Kyle had grown up to be. "The best way to start anything new is to commit it

113

to God. Maybe we should pray together and ask for his wisdom and help, then we can talk some more," she said.

After a prayer, they had a good talk about everything. At the end of it, they could all say they had learned a lot about each other and felt more comfortable knowing they could talk about any new questions that came up.

The next day, Mr. Clarkson was glad to have something specific to tell Marti's dad when he called looking for advice about Billy Joe's impending visit. The fathers agreed their daughters should not go out with boys as unescorted couples. They both felt it would be best to limit dating plans to events where the couples would go out with their group of friends who'd been together through so many experiences growing up.

The next afternoon, as he was waiting for Billy Joe to come over for dinner, Paul Philips prepared a hearty fire in the living room hearth. "Visual aids. Hm-m-m, that's the key," he said as he arranged the kindling.

Marti wanted to meet Billy Joe outside, before he walked into the house where her parents were putting the final touches on dinner. She took her time putting Bobcat in his stall until she heard Billy Joe's motorcycle coming down the road. She walked over to the gate slowly, timing it so she'd be sure to catch him before he rang the doorbell.

Billy Joe never rode his bike over the speed limit, but if a state trooper stopped him that night, it would have been for going too slowly. He wanted one more chance to go over what to say to Mr. Philips. When he'd asked Pastor James about what to do, the older man who had been like a father to him for so many years got out a roll of duct tape and tore off two pieces. He gave the whole roll of tape to Billy Joe to keep, along with some good advice.

Marti saw the motorcycle finally pull into the long driveway and waved. She smiled as he stopped short and turned off the motor. "You're early," she said as he took off his helmet.

"Well, I sure didn't want to be late," he answered nervously. "And I hoped you might still be out here."

Marti grabbed his hand. "I just wanted to say, well, thank you for being patient and waiting for my answer about the dance."

"Oh, I totally understand. I mean, you shouldn't feel like you have to answer that kind of question immediately. I just hope I didn't put any pressure on you by the way I asked or anything. Like I said, I've never done this before, so, uh . . ."

"Oh, no. It was fine. I was just surprised, that's all."

"Well, that's a relief. I told Pastor James about it and he said he better not hear anything bad about me. He's a great guy. I'm lucky to have him in my life. He gave me some good advice about everything."

"Oh, cool. What was the advice?"

"Ah, let me tell you first and you can tell me if it's the right thing to say to your parents, okay? I want to make sure I get this right."

"Okay, let's hear it."

Billy Joe got the roll of duct tape out of his jacket pocket. He unrolled a piece of it and tore it off. "You see how sticky the glue is on this piece of duct tape? That's because it's never been stuck to anything yet. And that's how duct tape is supposed to be. It's one of the best things you can use to hold two things together. It bonds to whatever you stick it on and it's really difficult to get it off."

"Uh, sure. That's really interesting, but . . ."

"I'm not finished." Billy Joe fished in his jacket pocket again and found a smaller piece of the tape. It was covered with lint. He held it up. "Touch the sticky side on this piece of tape."

Marti did. Her finger came away from it easily and the tape hung limply. Billy Joe looked triumphant. "See that. The tape barely stuck to your finger. That's because I stuck it to my sweater and then pulled it off six times."

Marti looked confused. Why were they talking about tape? "I see. Well, that's interesting, but . . ."

"Wait. I'm not finished. There's more: Your heart is like duct tape."

"It is?"

"Yes. Our hearts were meant to stick together the way fresh pieces of tape do. They were meant to form a bond that lasts forever. But if we go from person to person, trying out love, we do the same thing to our hearts that I did to the piece of tape that lost its stickiness. We get them all full of debris and, after a while, the glue

116
♪

won't hold on to anything in a strong way. That's what Pastor James warned me about. He said we have to be careful how far we let our emotions go and relationships go, so when we are ready to make a lifetime commitment to one person, our hearts will still be sticky. So what I want you to know, what I want to tell your parents, is that I am pledging to be a careful guardian of their trust and yours. I don't want to leave a bunch of lint on your heart because I wasn't careful or respectful toward you."

Marti's eyes sparkled with tears. "Wow! I never thought duct tape could be beautiful."

At that moment, her dad opened the front door and looked out at them. "Hey, I thought I heard a motorcycle. Come on in, you two. Dinner's ready. What's that? Tape? Did you break something on your bike?"

117

13

Back-to-School Special

S IMONE LOOKED at the clock in the lunchroom and decided she could squeeze in an extra twenty minutes of practice if she just grabbed an apple from the salad section and took it to the band room. She fidgeted in line until she got to the place where she could reach one—there—a nice, shiny Red Delicious. She plucked it from the bowl and sorted through her change as she waited to get to the cashier.

She could not believe how well everything had turned out after praying with Ben at the hospital. Adam and the band had been able to audition for the school band director at College Corner and help him out in a pinch—the one created by the ridiculous claims Doug

Wembly made when arranging for them to play there and be judged by the band director.

"Why Wembly thought we should be able to just pull pop tunes out of thin air without even asking us, I can't imagine," Adam told Simone, fuming in her hospital room after they got back.

"But we did it—no problem," Moby said, grinning and shaking his blond dreadlocks.

"Wembly heard our demo tape, so he could probably tell we had the skills," Conan said, tapping his drumsticks on the edge of Simone's hospital bed.

Greg nodded in time to Conan's drum solo, looking smug. "The band director said he was giving us his highest score. And the kids at the dance loved us, too."

The guys couldn't believe how well it had all gone. Simone was amazed. She had thought all was lost, but the next day she got a message from Wembly saying they were in the finals. One more live show with the judges attending would be next, and if they survived that round, they'd compete in New York against the final ten top bands for the grand prize. He was supposed to call this afternoon with details—where and when.

Simone felt much better about everything by the time her dad arrived at the hospital to drive her home. Poor Dad—he looked so worried and tired. Still no news from Mom, but he was still clinging to the belief everything would be fine. Maybe he was right. Everything worked out for the band without her help. Could it be her dad and Ben were right about waiting and praying?

119

It still didn't ring true in Simone's heart. She tapped her foot and twisted the stem on the red apple as she waited in line.

"Vat? Dat's all you haf?" Mrs. Owczarek, the lunchroom lady everyone called just "Mrs. O," interrupted Simone's thoughts.

"Oh, I've got to go practice. I'm not that hungry," Simone said, trying to press a handful of change into Mrs. O's hand for the apple.

Mrs. O shook her head and her ruffled blue hair cap hopped a little to one side. She threw the apple a disapproving look and explained in her thick Eastern European accent, "Yah, you aren't hungry now, hon. But dat's not enuf protein. You get low blood zuger. You vill fall asleep in class. Here," the older lady pulled a plastic-wrapped granola bar from the dessert counter and handed it to Simone. "You get dis one, too. Protein bar, just one dollar."

Simone rolled her eyes and grubbed a dollar from the bottom of her purse. She knew better than to argue with Mrs. O. It would get her out of the cafeteria faster if she just took the food than if she wasted time in a health discussion. Also, she knew Mrs. O was right, so why argue? The lunch lady beamed a big smile as she waved goodbye. *Well, I made her day anyway*, Simone thought. No wonder the lunch line moved like a snail on vacation, with a crusader like Mrs. O at the gate watching over everyone's dietary habits.

Simone was grinning as she slid around the corner on the shining wooden floor and through the big band room doors. Even though it could be a pain, Simone really loved Mrs. O and everyone like her who held out for something they believed in with a passion. She thought about her own passion for music and knew she did the very same thing to her band—always being a stickler for perfection and wheedling for "just one more run-through" on certain parts of their music. *Yep, I'm a pain to people when I do that, too,* she thought. But she didn't see any cure for it. *If you're passionate about a subject, you just have to hold people up sometimes and stop them from moving on to the next thing without finishing the first thing.* She wondered if a certain look she'd seen Adam give the other guys after she'd cornered them to make a small change to a piece of music was the same look she had just given Mrs. O. She was pretty sure it was. Well, right was right. She opened the crinkly wrapper on the granola bar and munched bites as she set up her practice room.

121

Twenty minutes later, Adam tapped on the practice room window. He had just finished lunch and knew where he'd find Simone.

"Guess who left a message on my cell? Our old pal Wembly," he said to Simone when she opened the door. "He said your phone must be turned off and wanted us to call right back because he has news from the contest."

Simone switched on her cell and there was a blinking message icon. She and Adam listened to the voicemail on speaker: "Hi, Simone. Doug Wembly here. Call me. I'm trying to set up another audition for your band. I have an idea for you."

She was about to return the call when Kyle tapped on the window. Adam opened the door and Kyle shook his finger at them, saying, "So, I just found out you two have been keeping a secret from your best friends. You're busted. Tell me everything."

Simone looked shocked, and she was. "What exactly do you think we're hiding?"

"Not showing up for Bible study, and having secret practice sessions without Michelle and Teri? I should have guessed. It was pretty embarrassing to have to hear it from some stranger!"

"All right, what did you hear?" Adam demanded, wondering how Kyle could have heard anything about their band. Was that what he was talking about, or something else?

"I'm on the committee for the dance and we got a call from the director of a band contest wanting to know if your band could play a couple of songs there for the competition. He said it would really help you out because you have to perform in front of a live audience. He said he'd send judges and it would give our school lots of great publicity or something."

"Wembly!" Simone and Adam said together.

"Yeah, that was his name. So this guy is for real?" Kyle took off his glasses and crossed his arms, blocking the doorway. "You two better give me the whole story."

They told Kyle about how it had gone for them so far—even including the part where Simone saw her mom. Telling everything aloud to someone who hadn't been there, it did sound like a strange tale, but if anyone could understand what was going on, Kyle would. He looked at them a minute, adding the whole thing up.

"Well, that's another piece of the puzzle I didn't have. So our town isn't the only place where there are Angel Lines. What you don't know is how much this connection to Paris makes sense. We found out Angela's uncle saw her Aunt Candace from the Paris Opera House when the Angel Line in her hospital room opened. It must have been a trick that Clé guy was using, because Candace didn't go to Paris when she saw her husband. Somehow Clé made her go to the cabin here in town so he could add her as one of his hostages instead."

"Are you saying I actually went to Paris?" Simone asked. "I didn't just faint and have a dream?"

123
♪

"Wait a minute," Adam said, shaking his head. "That doesn't make sense. You were there on the grass at the golf course. You didn't disappear. I saw you the whole time."

"No," Simone said, looking confused. "You and the guys and the golf course were the ones who seemed to disappear . . ." She sat down and put her chin in her hands.

Kyle got out his PDA and typed in some notes. They had to solve this new mystery. "Well, The Lines may be opening up again. I don't know why. Maybe that old golfer guy made something happen messing around near the black stones with his golf club. Maybe it's something going on at that area because of those ancient mounds and you just happened to be there. But, Simone, your mom is in Paris, and you said the reason you entered this band competition was to win the prize to go there. That's a strong connection. It seems to me the best way to find out more is to keep following this path."

Simone looked up, her eyes dancing with hope. "You mean we're going to get supernatural help? Win the contest? Could that be why I saw an angel playing music in my dream?"

"No way I can guess. But I do think you should agree to Welby's plan and see where it leads."

"Wembly. I'll call and tell him we'll do it," Simone said, picking up her cell phone.

"Yeah, and next time you hold a Bible study, we'll be there, too," Adam said, patting Kyle on the shoulder as he left. "We don't want to miss what you guys find out and we don't want you to miss any of the puzzle pieces we find."

14

The Dance

W OW, YOU LOOK, uh, great," Kyle stuttered. It was safe to say Angela had never seen a boy look at her with that much admiration. She didn't know what to say about it. She decided to turn the compliment back to him.

"Not bad yourself!" she laughed, hoping it could put them both at ease. But the compliment was deserved. In a suit, Kyle looked much older and, anyone would admit it, he looked handsome. "Do you think our friends will recognize us?"

"Maybe not," he said and visibly relaxed as they joked around. "Let's see if Marti and Billy Joe are fooled."

Aunt Candace made them pose for one photo together before they left, which they secretly enjoyed even though they protested that they'd be late, that posing arm-in-arm was silly, etc. It had been a lot of work getting dressed up and they agreed they might as well have a photo to remember it by.

Angela and her mom had shopped the weekend before for her dress. It was easy to tell that her aunts wanted to come along to the mall as they waved good-bye from the porch, but they had agreed this trip was the ultimate mother/daughter day. She and Mom had visited every store and tried on dozens of dresses before they narrowed it down to three. They sent cell phone pictures to Aunt Chloe, Aunt Candace, Michelle, Teri, and Marti for votes. The final choice was a midnight blue gown with silver trim around the neckline and waist.

"You look like a starry night!" Mom exclaimed. She insisted on getting matching silver shoes, even though Angela felt guilty buying the fancy footwear she couldn't imagine using anywhere again. When Mom and the aunts finished putting her hair in an updo with a dark waterfall of spiraling curls, she felt like a princess.

She continued holding onto Kyle's arm after the picture had been snapped and let him walk her to Marti's car. It felt weird but, as she explained it to herself, it was a good idea since she walked a bit wobbly in her slippery dress shoes, even though the heels were not all that high. *Could I ever get used to any of this?* she thought, as she tried to keep pace with Kyle. She remembered her dad's advice to stay out of Kyle's way in case he wanted to open the car door for her. He did.

The Dance

Billy Joe was in the driver's seat and Marti looked out the passenger window with an expression of such surprise that Angela half expected her to throw her hands up against the glass for effect. Thankfully, she didn't do that. When Kyle bent to open the back door for her, however, Marti silently mouthed, "You look great!" and Angela could feel a blush bursting onto her cheeks. Teri and Chuck were already in the backseat. Tall, blond Teri looked like a million bucks in a black velvet gown. She scooted over to make room for them and said, "Wow, Angela! That dress is amazing."

Angela didn't know what to say. *Oh, boy! This is going to be a long night.*

Angela wasn't the only one thinking about the difficulties this night could bring. Adam was actually thinking the exact same words while Simone had the band go over the song intro one more time before leaving for sound check at the school. *This is going to be a long night.*

"How perfect does perfect need to be, Simone?" Moby complained, raking his fingers through his blond locks.

She gave him a look that sizzled and he decided not to press for an answer. Simone knew she was pushing it from the glum looks the band members wore, but she just couldn't stop worrying. She knew they could do better if they just tried it one more time . . .

"That's it," Adam said when he realized she was about to ask for another run-through. "Time's up. Let's go."

127
♪

He pulled the neckstrap to his baritone over his head and started packing it in the case. Everyone else jumped to follow his lead, avoiding eye contact with Simone. She sighed. Her friend was right. It was time to do their best and hope for the best. She bent over her case and packed up her sax.

The plan was for Blueberry Koffee to play three songs during the scheduled band's break. Judges from the contest would be there to hear them and gauge audience reaction, etc. Instead of hiding their band, Adam and Simone started telling everyone to come and support them. The school newspaper did a story on their progress in the contest so far and the local newspaper picked it up as front-page news. Of course, Moby, Greg, and Conan's friends were coming, including their girlfriends. They put up some posters at Taste of Heaven to promote it as well.

"I think we have a good chance of winning," Moby had said, tacking his artsy poster to the wall behind the coffee counter.

Everyone just stood back and looked at it. He had designed it like an album cover and their black-and-white band photo made them appear much cooler than any of them felt. Now Simone just hoped people who saw it wouldn't think it was false advertising.

They could hear the official band for the dance from the band room—loud and trendy pop music with a little rock thrown in. Simone started to get nervous about playing jazz music after listening to them for a while.

Adam was confident. "Don't worry, Simone. We'll be playing during that group's break. It'll be like an intermission anyway, so anyone who doesn't want to listen can go to the courtyard for a break or to the cafeteria for snacks."

The double doors to the band room sprang open and Kyle burst in. They almost didn't recognize him with his suit and styled hair. "Everyone ready to go?" he asked, looking excited. "Great. I'm going to introduce you. The two judges from the contest are already in there. One of them said they already saw you play at College Corner."

"Is it the band director from the high school?" Greg asked.

"No, they're both from New York. He said they watched you on a tape the band director at that school made."

Just then Angela, Teri, Marti, and Michelle came through the doors to wish them luck. Simone could not believe how dazzling her friends looked in their gowns. She suddenly felt a little underdressed in her simple black pants and dark blue silk shirt.

"You look great," Teri said, giving her a hug. "You chose the right colors for the leader of Blueberry Koffee. That silk shirt is very jazzy."

"It's amazing to see you all dressed up," Simone said, hugging each one and trying not to crush their dresses or smudge their makeup or muss their hair.

As they were leaving, two thirty-something men came through the door. It had to be the judges. They looked very New York-ish and very music star-ish, with trendy suits and hair. The clipboards gave them away, too. The taller of the two introduced himself first. "I'm Doug Wembly, and you must be Simone," he said. Flashier than Simone had pictured him, Wembly smoothed back his sculpted black hair and trained his startling blue eyes on her before introducing his tall, blond friend, who removed his sunglasses briefly and nodded. "This is Eric Vansel, our head judge. You'll remember him as the lead singer from Broken Heart."

Simone had no idea who Eric Vansel (or Broken Heart) was, but smiled and wished she could say something good about the group or proclaim one of their hits her favorite song. She wondered if it would hurt his feelings if she didn't ask for an autograph or something. "It's great to meet you," was all she could think of to say.

Fortunately, Moby had heard of the band. "Wow, I can't believe you came out to our little school to hear us. One of the first albums I bought in grade school was by Broken Heart."

Eric Vansel smiled, then spoke with an English accent and a slight lisp, "Thanks. Always good to meet a fan."

Simone introduced Adam, Conan, and Greg.

Wembly wrote some notes on his clipboard, and then turned to go. "We'll be in the audience and meet back here to talk with you afterward."

It was time. They carried their instruments to the stage and found Kyle nervously waiting to go out with them. "My voice is going to crack, I know it," he whispered to

Simone. She just stared at him as if he were speaking
Martian. She was already playing the music in her head
and clicking the keys on her saxophone.

Kyle rushed up on the stage ahead of them and
adjusted the microphone to his height. "Thanks so much
to Rockit Science. Let's give them another hand," he said,
letting go of the mike stand to clap. He caught the stand
a split second before it fell, and continued his intro.
"While Rockit Science takes a break, we have something
different for you to enjoy. You might have read my arti-
cle in the school paper about the band contest Simone
Leuw and Adam Evans have entered with their band,
Blueberry Koffee. This is the last of three live perfor-
mances they're doing for the competition, so let's all give
them our support. C'mon everyone." Kyle started clapping and most of the kids in the audience joined in.
Some of the older kids started to leave and Simone's heart
fell. *I just hope we keep a big enough audience for the judges.*

"A fit audience, if few," Kyle whispered in her ear,
patting her shoulder as he left the stage. "Like Milton."

Milton who? Simone wondered, *Paradise Lost* the fur-
thest thing from her mind. Anyway, it was more than just
a few who stayed to hear them play. She expected only
polite applause after the first piece, but the whole marching band had stayed and they clapped and cheered, led on
by their director, Mr. Sandler. The dynamic music teacher
was Simone's favorite, and even more so after he jumped
up and whistled the minute the music stopped. He did the
same for the next piece and the audience stayed with him.

131

"Thank you all so much. This last song is one I composed for the competition," Simone announced, feeling shy as her voice echoed through the mike. Mr. Sandler absolutely beamed, his fuzzy goatee stretched out like a shadow underlining the big smile he threw her. She wished she'd been brave enough to tell him about her secret entry from the start, but he didn't seem at all disappointed. *Okay. Here goes.* She counted down for "Raindrops in Moonlight."

It couldn't have gone more smoothly. As she played, Simone imagined the feeling of the rain, saw her mom, lost her, and found her again. It was like a prayer set to music. And it was also a question—one that only solving the mystery of her mom's disappearance could answer. When she stopped playing, everyone was silent for about four beats. Then they cheered.

15

Aftermath

BLUEBERRY KOFFEE took several bows as the room exploded in applause. Simone hugged each band member, starting with Adam, and wiped tears of joy from her eyes. Mr. Sandler leaped up onto the stage and hugged Simone and Adam together. "I'm so proud of you both," he yelled over the crowd's noise. All their friends were yelling "Awesome! You rock!" and waving from the floor of the gymnasium.

The band had to take down all their equipment as quickly as possible because Rockit Science needed to get back on stage, so there wasn't time to talk to their friends. "Let's get our stuff put away and we can relax and have fun with everyone else," Adam said into Simone's ear. "Maybe we'll show them that saxophone players can dance, too."

She looked at her friend and smiled—the happiest smile he'd seen from her in a month. "Okay!" her lips said, though it was too noisy to hear her words.

While the guys put their equipment in their cars, Simone decided to put hers in her band room locker and meet Wembly as planned. She hadn't seen him since the performance. He and his companion seemed to have disappeared from the back of the room the minute the performance ended.

As she started to open the door to the band room, Simone was almost knocked over by someone throwing it open from the inside. A man's angry voice yelled, "This is your problem. Deal with it yourself!" and Eric Vansel burst through the door. He stopped when he saw Simone's startled face and tried to put on a more friendly expression. "Excuse me. That was a wonderful performance. You are a very talented young lady." He looked like he was about to say more, but he just shook her hand and said "Good luck" before hurrying away. What did that mean? Good luck in the final round?

She went into the band room and saw Doug Wembly fumbling with his clipboard as if about to write on it. "Simone, there you are. I was just going to leave you a note. I figured you'd be busy with your fans. That was an exceptional performance out there."

"So are we in the finals?" she asked, smiling hopefully. She didn't see how they could miss after the performance had gone so well.

"Uh, I want to talk to you about that. There was some misunderstanding on Eric's part about what he was coming here to see. He had only seen the tape of the band playing pop songs at the high school in College Corner. They looked and sounded a lot more like the other two bands we've chosen. Your guys are really good. Seeing them play with you tonight, I realize they were just fooling around at that dance. You are all great. Really. And that's the problem."

"How so?" Simone felt confused. *How could being good be a problem?*

Wembly shifted from one foot to another and looked at his notes. "This is a band contest, not a talent contest per se. It's about a band being a viable commodity—a product, so to speak. You and your band are like a pair of silver dress shoes, but what our shoppers want are beach sandals. Get what I mean? Our audience is kids—they just want some light, fun music they can dance to. I thought you were too good for us when I saw your first audition tape, but I wanted you to get a chance to perform at least once—maybe raise the bar a bit for the others. When I saw the tape from College Corner, I thought you'd changed style—so much so, that I thought you could win against the others. That's why I brought Eric here."

"So we're out of the competition?" Simone's heart sank. She felt sick.

"I'm sorry, Simone. But if you heard the other two bands, you'd understand. They sound just like that." He

135

nodded toward the sound of Rockit Science coming from the hallway. "A tad more experienced, but basically the same. They're just not in the same ballpark as your band."

Simone sat down on a folding chair. Wembly was really sorry. He tried to cheer her up by saying, "Look, I know of a couple of other contests for bands with your style and talent. The prize for one of them is a scholarship to a great music college and the other has a trip to study at the Jazz Institute in New York City. I'll e-mail you the info on them, okay?"

"Sure, thanks," Simone nodded. He didn't get it. She watched as he turned his back and left. She stared at the door as it swung shut behind him. She couldn't have explained to him the reason she had no interest in other contests right now. She felt relieved when the room was empty.

Simone shoved her sax into its black nylon gig bag and zipped it up. So that was it. She had missed her chance to go on the tour and look for Mom. Back to waiting and hoping.

She sat there alone, avoiding the rest of the band and the friends who'd be waiting in the gymnasium to tell her they thought she should have won. That had never been the point, but she had to admit, the thought of winning had taken root in her mind. She felt her work could stand up to anyone else's in the competition. But who could say which music was better? Which work was "worthy" of the prize depended on who was doing the listening.

In front of a crowd of teenagers who just wanted to dance, her music was probably too complicated and not repetitive enough. The music biz guys were tuned in to what their crowd would buy, not looking for a band who drew a few cheers from an audience of bandies.

Simone had guessed wrong. She had worked too hard. She could feel her heart breaking.

She sat down on the floor next to her sax case, dropping her head into her hands. Disappointment drowned her other emotions like a flood, until it was almost too much effort to breathe. *Now what, God?*

Suddenly she heard the exit door behind her open, letting in a slight breeze from the wintry air outdoors. She breathed in the refreshing scent of pine trees and heard a sound like tiny bells jingling. She looked up to see who'd come in, hoping she wouldn't have to talk about what had just happened. Surprisingly, it was Mrs. Owczarek, the lunchroom lady, who briskly entered the room as if to pass through on her way to another part of the school. She dropped the set of keys she'd just used to open the door into the pocket of her blue smock, then turned to look at Simone as if just as surprised to see her there.

137
♪

"Vell, vat are you doing here?" she asked. "Party is in dah big room, hon."

"Hi, Mrs. O," Simone sighed. "I know about it. I just finished playing. I was putting my instrument away."

"Ah, vell, I'm sorry I missed dah music," Mrs. O said, looking genuinely sorry about it. "Vat instrument you got dere?"

Simone opened the music case and the older lady's eyes grew round with interest. "Can you play a little for me? Please?"

There was no reason not to, Simone decided. She didn't have anywhere to go. She picked up the sax and put it together in a blink. She thought for a second about what she'd play, and then chose a simple waltz melody she'd learned years ago.

Mrs. O closed her eyes and a broad smile bloomed on her face. The way she pursed and unpursed her lips almost looked as though she were tasting the music. "M-m-m-m. Dat's goodt."

As Simone played, Mrs. O began to wave one hand as if directing an invisible orchestra sitting in the middle of the band room. Simone looked across the room and thought her eyes must be watering. The floor where Mrs. O's invisible orchestra would be sitting grew blurry in the center as if it were melting into ripples. The ripples became wider and wider until they seemed to reach all the way to Simone's feet. She blinked rapidly, but it didn't change what she saw. Maybe she was fainting or something? The walls on the other side of the room became all rippled, too, as if melting into liquid.

She stopped playing and wiped the back of her hand across her eyes. Nothing changed. She was looking at a body of water where the floor used to be and even more water where the walls across the room used to be! She took a step back as the edge of the "water" touched the tips of her shoes and wet marks appeared on them. She looked up at Mrs. O in shock.

"Vell, vell," the lunch lady said and smiled, "guess it's time to go . . ."

At that moment, the door opened again and Madame Corbeau bustled in from the hallway, wrapping a long black shawl across her shoulders. "Sorry! Sorry, I'm late, Halina," she called to Mrs. O. "But I see you managed without me."

"It vas Simone's music," Mrs. O explained. "She hardly played at all and the vater came to her."

"What are you talking about? What is going on?" Simone asked, pointing at the water.

"It's time to go, dear," Madame said gently. "You want to find your mom, don't you?"

"My mom? What's my mom got to do with . . ."

"There's more than one way to cross the ocean," Madame said mysteriously. "You prayed for a way to get to her, correct? Well, here you go. A way through the midst of the sea."

This was too much for Simone. "What are you saying? This is the Atlantic Ocean? And how am I supposed to cross it? Are you going to part it or something?"

"Oh, ha, ha, silly girl. Of course not, ve just valk on it," Mrs. O said, waving a hand and smiling brightly. With that, she put one foot out over the water. Before she could put her shoe on the liquid, however, dozens of small, silver fish swarmed up to the surface and formed a shimmering path in front of her. The lunch lady reached into the big pockets of her smock and pulled out hand-fuls of what looked like breadcrumbs. She cast them out in front of her and the silver path grew. When she stepped on it, the cloud of tiny fish seemed to hold her up, just on the water's surface.

"Lovely, Halina!" Madame exclaimed, and then she took Simone's hand. "Come, *chérie*, we have to hurry before the path melts."

Simone saw that the little, silver fish were swarming to hold Madame Corbeau's shoes at the surface of the water just as they had done for Mrs. O. She decided this was either a dream or a miracle. No matter which it was, she could see it was working, so she gave it a try. As soon as the shadow of her shoe fell across the water's surface, the path became solid with little fish. As she gradually put her weight on it, the silvery path became even firmer and held her up. It wasn't slippery—*Another miracle,* she thought, *considering it's made of fish.* It almost felt like beach sand. It gave slightly with her weight, but distributed itself evenly with each of her steps, just like wet sand would.

"Oh, this feels wonderful," exclaimed Madame. "It's so soothing to my feet after walking on those hard tiles at school. How lovely! Just like a cloud."

"Yah, now my little friends are happy. Dey have been vaiting to play a part in our adventure for so long, haven't you, pretties?" Mrs. O said as she sprinkled a few more crumbs to the fish.

"Yes, all creation yearns to be a part of the revealing of the children of God," Madame agreed.

"What do you mean?" asked Simone.

The tiny lady turned her twinkling blue eyes to the girl and said, "It is their privilege to help with your journey, to be specially chosen to help with God's plan."

That was a confusing statement to Simone. "Are you saying that all that has been going on is God's doing? Did God make it so my mom couldn't come home?"

"Not at all—just the opposite. God's plan is to bring her back to you. She became part of his company to set the captives free, and now it is time to help her complete her mission—by completing yours!"

"Wait! What are you talking about? What do you know about the company my mom works for?" Simone was pretty sure her usual policy of neither confirming nor denying wasn't going to work with ladies who could walk on water. As she looked down at the shimmering pathway, it seemed like a good time for complete honesty with her traveling companions.

"Vee know all about it. Vee are all part of the same company," said Mrs. O, throwing Simone a very knowing wink.

"That's right," Madame Corbeau agreed, nodding.

"You? You're agents?" asked Simone incredulously.

"That's correct, my dear. We have been assigned to look out for you during your mother's mission. But we could not tell you about it until now. Until it was time to

141
♪

allow you to join the company," said Madame, looking at Simone very seriously.

"You want me to be an agent?" Simone could not believe it. Was she old enough for a top secret clearance? Maybe age had nothing to do with it . . .

"Age has nothing to do vith it," said Mrs. O as if answering Simone's thoughts.

The shimmering path was closing behind them and opening in front of them as far as her eyes could see. It was as if all the tiny, silver fish in the ocean were scurrying to get in on the line.

"I've never seen so many fish on the path," Madame said, shading her eyes as if to see the end of it. "The sea is like glass tonight, so maybe I just hadn't been able to tell how far they extended before."

Now Simone was really shocked. "You do this a lot?"

"Only ven God makes our path straight," Mrs. O said, smiling as if that explained everything.

"It's confusing if you think about it too hard," Madame explained when she saw the expression on Simone's face. "God's travel has more to do with timing than with time. When the timing is right, he makes our path a straight line, no worries about the curvature of the earth or the hills and valleys. It's just straight to the heart of the matter, so to speak, in as short or long a time as is necessary—so we begin and arrive at just the right time."

"Huh? Yeah, well, now it's perfectly clear," Angela joked, rolling her eyes and laughing. But there was something so true about what Madame had said. Even though it was the strangest path she'd ever walked, she didn't feel afraid. She felt right—as if she belonged to the path and it belonged to her. It all felt impossibly right. "But if this is not a dream, it's a miracle."

"Oh, dah vorld is full of miracles. And ve are miracles to dah rest of the vorld," Mrs. O said, throwing out another sprinkling of breadcrumbs to the tumbling swarm of tiny fish.

Madame pointed to the shimmering path. "The Angel Lines are straight paths between sacred places where angels and ancient people met to worship and serve the one true God. Long ago the paths opened in season, when it was God's timing for people to gather. Things didn't start out like they are today. Now we rush to and fro under our own power, and we make our own calendars and plans to please ourselves, without even wondering if they will please God."

"Yah, ve even tell God ven it can be time for church or ven it is time to pray. People decide dat for themselves— like God should vait for them to give him an appointment. It's all backvards."

"Or we act like he should hurry up because we are tired of waiting," Madame added.

Simone blushed. It sounded like Madame had been listening to her impatient, worried thoughts.

As she looked away, she noticed the horizon, below the moon and shining stars. It had held only a vista of dark blue water, but that was changing. Simone could see

143
♪

a dark fringe of land appearing, lit from behind by a glow of silver light. It was still fully night—nowhere near sunrise, and the light looked coldly artificial, not warm like gathering dawn. Simone guessed the glow was from manmade light. A city? She glanced back at Mrs. O and Madame, who smiled as if they knew the answer and were just waiting for her to ask the question. "Is it . . . France?"

"Yah, yah, you see it already," Mrs. O laughed, clapping her hands in delight. "Ve valk dere much faster than flying in a plane."

"We are coming in under starlight," Madame said softly. "Our entrance will need to be secret."

"Why?"

"Your mother is expecting you, but she asked us to keep you as hidden as possible, dear. She was still looking into a mystery when last we spoke and she didn't know what danger she might find. But don't worry, there is a place prepared for you."

That was all Madame would tell her about their destination and her conversation with Simone's mother. They saw the shoreline grow, and it seemed to wrap around them until the ocean became more like a river. Houses and trees lined the shore, and then houseboats appeared along the banks. The floating houses looked so cozy with small, glowing lights and smells that promised wonderful foods cooking inside—probably in tiny kitchens, Simone imagined. She wondered how long it had been since she'd eaten anything. Maybe Madame and

Mrs. O were wondering the same thing, because they soon walked up on a rocky beach area and waved good-bye to the silver swarm of fish that disappeared like a Fourth of July sparkler fizzling out. They walked up a cobblestone street and stopped in front of a small restaurant with a sign over the door that read *La Lune*. Simone swayed a little, getting her legs adjusted to standing on firm land as she peered through the shining restaurant window. Everywhere people sat chatting and eating at the small, round tables. The land felt so solid under her feet after walking on the fish path for so long, it was almost as if it were pushing back against her soles.

Madame held the door open and Mrs. O led the way. Simone picked up her feet and walked, somewhat ducklike, through the door. A round, dark-haired man in a white apron threw his hands up in the air and then rushed over to them, smiling and exclaiming, "Madame Corbeau, Mrs. O, you return to us!"

145
♪

"Bonsoir, Henri," Madame said cheerfully as the man kissed the air near each side of her face and then did the same for Mrs. O. Madame Corbeau gestured toward Simone, then said, "*Je vous présente notre amie Simone.*"

"*Enchanté, enchanté, Mademoiselle.*" Henri ducked his head in a courteous bow. "Come. You must allow me to give you our special table and our best meal."

Henri led them to a corner table separated from the rest of the tables by a row of plants in brass pots on one side, with a view of the street out the big window on the other side. He brought them a platter that held several kinds of cheese, fruit, and a basket of fresh bread. Simone couldn't guess whether it was from the long walk or the ocean air, but she suddenly felt very hungry. She could not believe how wonderful each piece of cheese tasted and how fragrant the bread smelled. "Gruyère, camembert, chèvre . . ." Mrs. O chanted as she tasted each variety of cheese.

"*Bœuf bourguignon à la maison*," their host announced when he placed bowls of dark, rich stew on their table. It was full of vegetable pieces and the most flavorful, tender beef Simone had ever tasted. As she ate one spoonful after another, she started to feel its warm glow spreading from her full stomach to her fingertips. To ward off sleepiness, she began to look out the restaurant window.

146

♪

The dark street was not very busy. An occasional car with amber headlights or a group of people would pass by, but there was such a different feeling about the scene. Everything looked so much older than in her own town. The buildings were all made of stone and decorated with small statues at just about every corner. Their heavy wooden doors were weathered in a way that made her wonder how many times they had opened and shut, and how many people had passed through them over hundreds of years.

Then she caught sight of a familiar structure that made her drop her spoon back into her soup bowl and blink to make sure she really saw what she thought she'd seen. There was no mistake. It was the Eiffel Tower silhouetted in front of the moon.

16

The Shadow
of History

S IMONE POINTED out the window at the tall, triangular silhouette outlined by twinkling Christmas
lights and stuttered, "E-e-eiffel Tower?"

"Ah, Le Tour Eiffel. *Mais, bien sûr.* Of course, it's the
Eiffel Tower. You can see it from almost anywhere in
Paris," Madame said, smiling dreamily.

"So, we're in Paris? Already?" Simone was trying to
visualize the map of France she saw every day on the wall
in Madame's classroom. Paris was in the middle of the
country, not near the Atlantic Ocean. "I thought we were
in some little harbor town near the ocean."

Monsieur Henri had overheard her as he approached
the table. He made a sort of snort through his long nose

and frowned. "Mademoiselle, zis is Par-ee. And you are sitting in one of eets most famous cafés. La Lune was created from ze ruins of one of ze most beautiful cathedrals on ze banks of ze Seine."

"Please, Henri. We have finished our wonderful meal; would you show my student the ancient window?" Madame asked.

Henri seemed placated by this suggestion because the offended expression melted from his face. "Of course, my dear Madame." He beamed at the little teacher and nodded his head, almost bowing to her. Then he snapped his fingers to call a busboy, who came rushing at the command to clear their table. Henri elegantly pulled out the chair for Madame, Mrs. O, and Simone in turn, then he beckoned them to follow him. Holding the door to the restaurant open, Monsieur Henri began speaking as if talking to a tour group. "You cannot see our famous window from ze entrance. You must cross ze street and look at ze whole building."

They crossed the cobblestone street and looked back at the café. The building certainly didn't seem large enough to have ever been a cathedral, and it appeared too simple for such a title with its gray brick and simple carved stone accents framing the door and windows.

"Look at ze top window," Henri said, pointing to a window at the peak of the façade. Although it was the same gray stone, that window did not match the others. The design was more ornate. It looked as if it had been scorched; black stains as if from a fire smudged its surface in several places. Words had been carved across the top of the window, but Simone could not read them in French or English.

"Ze phrase on ze window, it is in Latin. It says 'After ze darkness, light.' See how ze moon is reflected in its glass? Ze light of ze moon comes after darkness, yes? But ze message goes more deep. Zere was once a beautiful church here zat was destroyed in ze revolution. Zis window was all zat was left. A very great darkness came to Par-ee, but now ze light returns."

Monsieur Henri put his hand on Simone's shoulder and smiled. She could see that the man thought this was an inspiring story, but it just sounded sad to her. How could building the old window into a new café make up for a church being burned down?

"Yah, vee vill see," Mrs. O said to Henri. "Light vants to return all right."

"Ah, you are all tired now," said Monsieur Henri, removing a key from a ring of old-fashioned keys attached to a gold chain hanging from his belt and handing it to Madame Corbeau. "You must rest at your lovely apartamont. Here is your key, Madame. I trust you will find everything in order zere."

"*Merçi mille fois* for taking care of my home for me, Henri," she said, patting his hand.

"*Mon plaisir*, Madame," he said, then turned to Simone and Mrs. O. "You vill enjoy ze view of Monsieur Rodin's garden. Ze roses still bloom, even in winter. *Au revoir, mes amies.*"

149

They waved as they walked away into the night and left Monsieur standing under the window with the moon shining over him like a beacon.

"It looks like a lighthouse," said Simone.

Madame laughed merrily, then said, "That it does; what a charming idea. It is somewhat of a lighthouse, and Henri is its keeper."

"Is it one of the links in The Angel Lines?" Simone wondered.

"Yes, a gateway, a very ancient one, into Paris. If you climbed up the stairs to the second story of his restaurant, you would find the seal of Charlemagne on the edge of that window. It is very old. Hardly ever used since the time of that great king. We are coming into Paris by the back door, so to speak."

Mrs. O pulled a blue scarf from her pocket and wrapped it over her head. "Ve hope no one vill notice us, yah?"

The three of them walked toward town, and it would be unlikely that passersby would remember them. Simone and Madame were as unnoticeable as shadows in their dark clothes and Mrs. O looked like any Parisian baker going home from a day's work. Anyone who saw them would never suspect them of the mission they discussed during their unusual journey or that their coming would set off a remarkable chain of events.

Simone had never taken a train ride in her life, but the Métro de Paris was about to change that. Madame took them to the entrance, where an ornate black railing and signpost marked the stairway that led down to the underground station. She pointed out the wall map of all the Métro lines that led to different places in Paris. "You never need a car in Paris if you learn the Métro system," Madame said, but Simone felt overwhelmed by the spiderweb of routes shown on the map; she was sure she'd have been completely lost trying to manage it alone.

Madame patted her hand. "You'd get used to it if you lived here for any length of time," she said, smiling contentedly and nestling into one of the train seats as if it were her living room chair.

"Yah, you get used to it, but still good to follow Madame. She does not get lost," said Mrs. O. "In Warsaw we also haf train everywhere. No need to park cars."

Simone slid in between the ladies. The train hummed along much more smoothly than her school bus, and its rhythm started to rock her to sleep. She shook her head a little to fend off the feeling and remembered a question she wanted to ask Madame Corbeau. "Monsieur Henri said the key he gave you was for your apartment, and you called it your home. Did you grow up there?"

"No, but my family lived nearby. My aunt Penelope lived in the apartment with my grandparents until they passed away. She ran her own business, a hat shop, just down the street. I used to work for her after school when I was old enough to help make hats. She was like a second mother to me and she left me the apartment in her will. I share it with family and friends when they visit the

151
♪

city. It's often empty nowadays until school lets out for summer and I return. Henri checks on it for me."

"An apartment in Paris . . . like a story in a novel . . ." Simone yawned. She leaned back in her seat as the train hummed along, jostling slightly side-to-side. Next thing she knew, her eyelids fell shut.

"Dah poor girl, she is azleep." The ladies smiled as they watched over her for a couple of stops, then Madame softly woke her.

"Time to wake up, Simone. This is our stop."

Simone opened her eyes, but everything looked like a dream. She walked between the two ladies, down a street, into a building, and up some steps, where they stopped at a green door. Madame inserted the key and opened it. The apartment was dimly lit and Simone was too sleepy to notice many details. Madame steered her toward a bedroom where Simone fell on the bed, her face buried in a feather pillow, dozing in an instant, fully clothed. She felt a heavy blanket cover her and someone pulled off her shoes and tucked the blanket under her feet.

As she drifted into a deeper sleep, she thought of something she had not considered until then—she hadn't brought a suitcase or any other clothes. She heard Madame and Mrs. O whispering and chuckling together. The sound grew fainter and a door shut behind them. That was the last thing Simone remembered as she fell into a sound slumber.

She didn't dream or stir until hours later when the sound of rain hitting the window next to her bed woke her. She lay there listening to it for a while, until the sound stopped altogether. She lifted her head and looked out the window to see that it was still night. One softly glowing street lamp illuminated the dark street. The rain had turned to a light mist with little flashes of light and rumbles of thunder in the distance. She remembered she was in Madame's apartment and how she got there, though the trip was a drowsy blur. She sat up, and then walked slowly to the window. She touched the old leaded glass, warped a bit with little air bubbles scattered throughout. The window had small rectangular panes welded together into a nine-foot-tall frame with an old-fashioned latch and no screen. The walls around it were made of weathered blocks of stone, like those in a castle. Simone gasped as the details of her recurring dream came back to her. When she heard footsteps approaching on the street below, she looked outside, knowing what she was about to see.

153
♪

Across the cobblestone street with its glistening coat of rainwater, the sound of footsteps came from opposite directions. Just as she had in her dream, Simone watched the tops of two black umbrellas appear out of the shadows. On the right, she heard the familiar tap of a woman's black high-heeled shoes as they moved out alternately from under the protective arch of her umbrella. On the left, there came the scuffing noise of a pair of men's brown oxfords stepping briskly across the cobblestones. As the two umbrellas passed each other they both made a little dip as if their owners had nodded a greeting to each other.

This time was a little different, though: Simone could see that the man held out a paper grocery bag with a long loaf of French bread sticking out of it. He gave it to the woman and it disappeared under her umbrella. Then the umbrellas continued on their separate ways and disappeared back into the darkness, leaving the street empty, shining silently in the mist. Simone's heart began hammering in her chest. She turned around, and there she saw the first door. Its wood grain looked like a face, but this time there was no moaning sound to frighten her. Instead, a note had been taped to the door. She went closer to read it:

The path of your dream is straight as the crow flies.

She recognized the handwriting, partly in script and partly printed—her mom's familiar way of lettering. The note was written on a little strip of paper, like the ones they put in fortune cookies, but Simone knew this was a secret message instead of a fortune. A message to let her know she could tell Madame her dream—Madame Corbeau, whose French surname meant "crow" in English. Had her mom been the last person to stay in this room? She looked around to see if Mom had left anything else. There was nothing much to see in the little bedroom, just a bed and a small dresser with an oval mirror.

In one corner there was a narrow closet door. She opened it. *Voilà!* Her mom had been there for sure. Simone could tell by the clothes hanging in the closet, Mom's own clothes Simone knew so well. It solved the no-suitcase problem she'd thought of as she fell asleep,

154

even if Mom's clothes would be a little big for her. There was a favorite gray sweater and black pants, a dark brown winter coat and knit hat, two pairs of jeans, and three long-sleeved tops. A little basket contained assorted socks and pajamas. A warm fleece robe hung on a hook, and a pair of sturdy black leather walking boots waited on the floor.

"Thanks, Mom," Simone said, deciding to change into the pajamas and robe for the remainder of the night, ". . . wherever you are!"

She pulled on some warm socks and thought she'd go see what there was to drink in the kitchen. She opened the door and stepped into the living room just in time to see the lock to the front door of the apartment turning to open. Someone in the outside hallway was unlocking the door to enter. Simone froze in place, unsure of what to do about this. The green door swung open and there stood Madame Corbeau with a paper grocery bag, shaking the rain off a big black umbrella as she folded it.

"Simone, you're awake," she said.

Simone stared at her like a zombie.

"*Are* you awake?" Madame asked as she saw the look on Simone's face.

"Yes, I was just dreaming about . . . well, it wasn't a dream this time. Did you go to the store in the middle of the night?"

"No, Henri met me and gave me some fresh bread and cheese for breakfast. After we left, he realized we wouldn't

have any food in the apartment, so he called and offered
to drop some by on his way to work at the restaurant."

"What time is it?"

"Very early morning. About five o'clock."

"Wow! I never get up this early."

"Well, your internal clock is probably off schedule.
You might want to have some herbal tea and try to sleep
a little longer."

Madame carried the grocery bag through a small,
arched opening into a cozy kitchen with yellow striped
curtains and wooden cupboards of light maple. She
turned on the gas burner under a copper teapot on the
old-fashioned stove, then opened a cupboard and brought
out a large glass jar filled with a colorful assortment of tea
bags. After setting the jar on a little wooden kitchen table,
she brought out two large white cups, the size of soup
bowls, and a small dish of light brown sugar cubes.

"Raw sugar in cube form," she said, smiling as she
opened one of the tea bags and put it in her cup. "Help
yourself to a tea bag."

Simone sat down and rummaged through the jar
until she found an orange herbal tea. Madame brought
the whistling teakettle to the table and poured steaming
water into both cups. The smell of oranges and herbs
from their cups hovered over the table. Simone decided
it was the perfect time to tell her dream to the "crow".

"I found a note from my mom on the bedroom
door," she began. Madame looked surprised. "Did you
know she had used the apartment?"

"Yes, but I didn't see the note. It must have been on the back of the door. What did it say?"

Simone got the folded paper out of the pocket of her robe and handed it to Madame, who read it, then chuckled. "Yes, I am the crow—that's what 'Corbeau' means . . . or the 'old crow,' as I've heard rumors some of my students call me. So, I guess your mom knows about your dream—the one you can't remember."

"I remember it now. The bedroom reminded me. It was in the dream—the windows, the street lamp. I saw you and Henri meeting outside the window with your umbrellas in the dream, and just now, too." Madame looked startled.

"You saw us?"

"Yes. The rain woke me and I looked outside just in time to see him hand you the bread. In my dream a face in the door talked to me, but here the note did the talking for my mom. Now I know it was her face I saw in the wood grain of the door. It's like she's trapped inside it and can't get out. The next thing I saw in the dream was a big, elegant, marble staircase with a brass rail. A brown dog was sleeping at the bottom, like a watchdog, but it didn't bark. There was a vase of pink tulips next to a heavy red door. I could hardly open the bolt, but when I did there was a garden outside and three nuns were walking around a circular path chanting, "Christ before me. Christ behind me. Christ in the heart of all who see me."

Madame looked excited. "There are many elegant staircases in Paris, but only one that I know of has a lazy

157
♪

watchdog and a red door at the bottom. Tell me more about the garden."

"It was outside the entrance to a large church, a cathedral or something. It had a rose window, the kind you told us about in French class. There was a secret door next to it and that's where the angel was playing music."

Simone told Madame the rest of the dream. The older lady listened intently, her eyes dancing as she nodded her head, encouraging the young woman to go on. When Simone had finished telling every detail of the dream as she remembered it, Madame got a pen and paper from a cabinet drawer and began to write.

"This dream is like a map. Somehow your mother knew you were dreaming it, because she told you to tell me about it. You begin here at my apartment. She may have left something else here for you to take with you."

"She left some of her own clothes in the closet."

"Ah, she is looking out for you, then. But check all the pockets carefully. Maybe there is more to it. Next we go to the youth hostel on Rue Fourcy. It has the staircase you saw, the red door, and the brown dog that watches but doesn't bark. I think we will find your mother there, or we'll find she left a clue as to where she is."

Now Simone was the one whose eyes were dancing. "Let's go, then. I'll never be able to sleep now!"

"Vee get up with sun," said a sleepy voice from the living room. Mrs. O pulled the drapes open and pointed to the glass balcony doors, where they could see a golden sunrise bubbling up. She came shuffling into the kitchen and poured herself some tea. "Monsieur Henri vas right. Dere really are roses blooming in Rodin's garden."

"Let's see," Madame Corbeau said, carrying her tea into the living room. She opened the balcony doors and stepped outside. Simone and Mrs. O joined her with steaming teacups. They stood in the crisp air and looked down into a beautiful garden with neat paths that wound around huge, stone sculptures. The paths were lined with rose bushes whose lush blossoms burst here and there in varying shades of red.

"I know some of these sculptures from your French class, Madame," Simone said. "That giant sitting with his head on one fist is 'The Thinker' and that big black door with all the scary creatures climbing around it is 'The Gates of Hell,' right?"

"Yah, I know dat one too," Mrs. O agreed. "And see how real red roses are blooming around it? Dat's something, huh?"

"Let's take it as a sign of hope for us today," Madame said as she held her hot tea in both hands, staring at the sculpture intently.

159
♪

17

Point of Interest

MADAME HAD said she knew of a youth hostel where the next door in Simone's dream was, and that Mom would be there or leave a clue there. In French class, they'd learned all about the youth hostels, hotels and houses that provided cheap or free places for traveling students to stay in cities throughout Europe. It made sense Mom was hiding there, because her writing assignment had been to research a book about hostels.

Before she chose a set of clothes to wear, Simone searched through the pockets for other clues. There were no more notes, but in a pocket of the coat she found something that could be even more useful. A large brass key, even older-looking and larger than the one to Madame's apartment. After putting on the gray sweater and black pants, Simone grabbed the walking boots and coat, carrying them along into the living room. In a full-length mirror by the front door, she stopped to stare at her reflection. Wearing Mom's clothes made her feel comforted, and now that she had them on, she could see why people said they looked alike. When she stood with her back to the mirror and glanced slightly over her shoulder, it looked just like Mom standing there. She felt both comforted and dismayed at the sight.

"We're coming, Mom," she whispered, then picked up her saxophone case and went into the living room.

Madame's voice called out from the other bedroom, "I think you've given us a plan for our travel disguise." Simone gasped as she saw the two ladies come into the living room. They were both dressed in black nuns' habits. "We won't be noticed as outsiders at the hostel or the cathedral in these," Madame explained.

"And people don't notice if you pray ven you are nun," said Mrs. O, placing the tips of her fingers together as if praying.

"Yes, we can stop and pray anywhere we like and no one will wonder about it. So you can do the same as long as you are with us. That's why we have these clothes in the first place. They come in very handy. For centuries this country was known as a spiritual haven, but after the French Revolution, many doors were locked to men and angels. The nation gave itself over to leaders who denied or doubted the existence of God," Madame told Simone

161 ♪

sadly. "It is now uncommon to see anyone pray outside of a church, and even inside of one, since so many have become museums rather than places of worship."

"They call France 'the graveyard of missionaries' because so many hearts vere hardened against Christianity," Mrs. O added.

"But faithful souls kept praying, sometimes in secret, and some doors are being opened once again," Madame said.

"Like the doors in The Angel Lines?" Simone wondered out loud.

"Yes. The Lines run from place to place on earth, but they also open to Heaven, and to Heaven's servants who come to answer prayer. Each link in The Lines has a link in the stars. The wheels of Earth line up with the wheels of Heaven," she said.

Mrs. O took a small Bible from a pocket in her nun's robe and held it up. "Like Ezekiel zays, 'A veel inside a veel' that turns to move God's chariot."

Simone had never heard anything like this. "So The Lines were for angels and people to travel on? People around the Earth, and angels back and forth from Heaven to Earth? Do people ever go to the stars on them?"

"Some have. Ezekiel, Daniel, John. They all saw the third Heaven."

"But stars are really suns. No one lives on them. Heaven is spiritual, isn't it?"

"Yah, you see with your eyes one thing and with your heart another. You hear music with your ears, but your heart hears another song," Mrs. O said, tapping her ear, then her chest.

Madame hugged her friend, then opened the front door and started outside.

"Oh, Halina, we could theorize all day and say the door to your heart is not in the heart that beats in your chest, but Simone knows that. Time to do something about it." Madame got out her key to lock the door behind them. That was when Simone remembered the key she had found.

"Look at this. We were talking about opening doors, and I found this key in my mom's coat pocket."

"Ah, von more puzzle piece for us!" Mrs. O said laughing.

"Keep it where you will not lose it. That key will come in handy today, if I'm not mistaken," Madame said smiling her usual mysterious smile. She took a necklace made of silver chain and pearl beads from around her own neck and strung the key on it, then gave it to Simone. "Prayer beads."

163
♪

They were the early birds on the streets of Paris that day. The sun sprang up fresh and golden as a summer peach. After the night's rain, everything shimmered in the dawn light as if it had been washed and polished. At first the three women were alone on the sidewalks as they passed the gates of the Rodin Museum mansion and walked toward the river.

Simone was fascinated to see the city in person after so many years of looking at slideshows and movies of its famous landmarks. It was so different to be there, her boots clicking across the cobblestones, than it had been to see it on a TV screen. The sounds of traffic, birds chirping, and people calling out to each other in French mingled with delicious aromas from bakeries and restaurants. The colors and textures grew as street vendors arrived and shopkeepers opened their doors to set out flowers, art, books, jewelry, and clothes. Statues and gargoyles leaned out from almost every building as if watching Simone and the ladies pass by. She pointed to a large one with froglike eyes and mouth that seemed to be looking right at them from a corner building.

"Madame, I remember that you taught us that the gargoyles were carved as decorations for the drain spouts that protect the buildings from rain damage, but it's just weird to see so many of them—they look like they are spying on us!"

"Don't worry about them," Madame said with a smile. "They were made to ward off evil with their scary faces, like jack-o'-lanterns. They look quite playful when it rains enough for water to come out of the spouts. They were carved at a time when people were more aware of the battle that rages between Heaven and Hell for our souls. The art they made reflected the belief that our fate does not end at our own fingertips, that we receive help from God or hindrance from his enemy on our journey here. Some of the statues are not water drains; they are statues of saints or angels, placed in alcoves around the buildings called *niches.* "

"You see angel and gargoyle facing each auder," Mrs. O said pointing to an angelic statue with hands in prayer across from the gargoyle that Simone had noticed. "Dey both haf jobs to do. Von scares off demons, von calls for angels to help."

"Is that why we say someone has found their niche when they choose a career or decide what subject to major in?" Simone asked.

"I imagine that is where the idea originated," Madame said. She gave Simone a little hug as they walked. "You are so clever, my dear Simone."

As they walked under the angelic statue, Simone glanced at it again. She thought it must have been an optical illusion that made the statue's head seem to nod toward its praying hands in agreement or blessing as the women moved on. They had to leave the wakening streets to take another Métro ride underground. Madame bought them all passes at the ticket kiosk and they took an eastward route for several stops, then left the train and came up a set of steps, back into the bright morning light and another surprise. Simone gasped.

165
♪

"It's Notre-Dame Cathedral—flying buttresses and all!"

"Yes, that's right, Simone. There she sits on her island in the middle of the Seine River, Île de la Cité, the island where the city of Paris was born. We're seeing the south side of Notre Dame as we approach, so you are right, those enormous winglike structures are the flying buttresses that hold the heavy stone and glass walls of the cathedral up from the outside."

"Vee haf to cross dah river here, den walk around dah church to get to Pont Marie, so we see Point Zero today," Mrs. O said.

"What is Point Zero?" Simone asked. It sounded familiar, but she couldn't remember what it was.

"Everyting in Paris starts dere," Mrs. O said and gave Simone a wink.

"Well, just as the city started here, the measuring of its growth starts here," Madame explained. "Each road and each point on the road is officially measured from this location, like spokes in a wheel. Most French cities have a point zero location, so the distance from city to city can also be measured from its center instead of from the border."

"Each city is like a wheel of its own? So is it that 'wheel within a wheel' again?" Simone asked.

Mrs. O patted her shoulder. "And not just cities . . . everyting is its own veel. Right down to dah cells and to atoms in dah cells. Vee are all turning together, yah?"

They crossed the "Petit Pont" bridge and turned right to face the front of Notre-Dame. As they walked up to its impressive entrance, Mrs. O pointed at a brass marker in the cobblestones with a star imprint in its center that looked like a small sundial. The shiny octagon was just large enough for Simone to stand on and fit both of her brown boots inside it. There was a larger paving stone shaped like a circle that surrounded the marker engraved with the words *Point Zero* and *Des Routes de France*. The round paver was divided into four parts, like a pie, and made the marker look more like a compass than a sundial. Simone felt sure she'd never have noticed it, mixed in with the cobblestones, if Madame and Mrs. O hadn't pointed it out to her. It made her think about The Angel Lines and how they connected to each other. Maybe Point Zero wasn't such a small thing as it looked.

Simone gazed in awe as they walked around the outside of the beautiful cathedral with its tall columns, statues, and immense colored-glass windows.

"You remember seeing photos of these windows in French class, don't you?" Madame asked.

"But it's so different seeing them in person," Simone answered. "I remember you said the windows and statues were made so people who couldn't read could still learn about history and the truth of the Bible by looking at the stories and symbols pictured in glass and stone. Now that I see how it would have felt to "read" the cathedral, I think that would be a great way to learn anything and everything!"

They walked on until they came to the end of the island and the bridge to Île St. Louis, the smaller island next to Île de la Cité in the middle of the river. Simone looked back to the first island and saw the tall spire of Notre-Dame in the distance pointing silently toward Heaven as it had been for centuries. They passed through the silent streets of Îsle St. Louis until they reached the Pont Marie bridge. There had been some early traffic as

167
♪

they left the Métro near the first bridge, but on the smaller island fewer people seemed to be awake this early. They crossed the north side of the river on Pont Marie bridge to return to the mainland on the opposite side from which they had started.

"We've crossed the Seine River that splits modern Paris," Madame said. "We started on the south side and now we are on the north side."

They continued north on the street that had been Pont Marie until its name changed to Rue Fourcy. Soon they came to a gray stone building with a strong wooden gate. The thick gate and towering walls made it look like a small castle to Simone, especially so because there were no windows on the first floor. She would not have been surprised to see a moat around it. There was only a sidewalk, however, with some small islands of grass and trees, so they easily approached the forbidding gate. As they did, Simone noticed there was a smaller door built into the left side of the gate. A sign on the wall next to it contained a notice that the door was not open until 8 a.m. Simone's heart sank. Would they have to wait a couple of hours to get inside?

Madame stepped up to the gate and pressed a button below the sign on the wall. Simone could hear a buzzing sound from inside, and soon she heard the sound of a latch on the inside jiggling and hinges turning. The small door creaked as it opened, and a beam of light poured out onto the shaded sidewalk. A woman's voice with a distinctly British accent called out in delight, "Madame Corbeau, Mrs. O, you are back!"

They stepped through the door into a sunny court-yard surrounded by walls and windows with a dozen wrought-iron bistro tables and chairs next to small trees. A sound of water pouring came from a three-tiered stone fountain in the middle. The tall woman who had opened the door stopped hugging Mrs. O long enough for Madame to introduce Simone.

"Madame Oursine, this is Simone."

Madame Oursine wore a wool coat with a big, brown fur collar that made her ample figure look even larger and taller. Her dark brown eyes and hair matched the fur collar.

"So you are Mandy's daughter. I'm so happy to meet you. Your mother and I are friends as well as fellow workers," she said. She looked about the same age as Simone's mom and it felt comforting to meet this friend who might finally lead them to Mom.

"Is my mother here?"

A worry wrinkle formed across Madame Oursine's brow. "She is staying in one of our rooms, but she has been gone for several days now. Come, and I will show you what she was working on."

They followed her through a large common room filled with long tables and benches where several people in black shirts and pants covered by red aprons were setting out breakfast. Madame Oursine picked up a plate of chocolate croissants that appeared to be fresh from the oven and offered them each an irresistible treat. Madame Corbeau helped herself to a small cup of coffee from a

169
♪

carafe as if she were in her own kitchen and poured two more for Mrs. O and Simone.

"I know. You said you don't drink coffee," she said, holding out the tiny cup to Simone. "But this is an espresso—dark and rich with no cream or sugar, and it's a perfect compliment to the sweet chocolate and butter in the croissant. Try just a sip after you eat some croissant."

Simone agreed to try a taste, and picked up a bottle of water to carry along as well, sure she'd need it to wash the coffee away. They carried the impromptu second breakfasts with them, following their host up a back staircase off the big kitchen and into a small office on the second floor.

"Sit down. Please make yourselves comfortable," she said, sitting down in a high-backed chair covered in rich, red velvet. It stood behind an ancient wooden desk with carved legs that looked like lion paws. Several heavy desk drawers rumbled contentedly as she rolled them open to rummage through their contents.

The three visitors were only too happy to sit in similar chairs across from the desk and nibble on their treats. They had taken a long walk in cold weather and the warm office chairs felt wonderful. Mrs. O sighed in satisfaction as she stretched out her legs and took a sip of coffee. Simone was happy to put her saxophone case down for the first time since they started walking from the Métro. She had to admit the dark, slightly bitter coffee enhanced the chocolate pastry's flavor. It was good and hot, and her eyes watered a little from the steaming contrast to the cold morning air she'd just left. She nodded at Madame to let her know she agreed with her recommendation on the drink.

Madame Oursine finished pulling items from the drawers and said, "So, here are the pictures from the Louvre. We were there last week looking at the relics from the twelfth-century castle below its foundation—Madame Corbeau probably taught you how the museum was built on the ruins of King Philip Augustus' castle, *n'est-ce pas?*"

Simone wanted to agree, but she actually could not remember that tidbit of trivia. *If Kyle were here he'd be able to remember it,* she thought.

Madame Corbeau gave her student a knowing look and made an excuse for her. "That was in last year's curriculum, and it wasn't on the final exam. They discovered the castle when they started renovating the museum in 1983, so it was before your time—you couldn't have seen it on the news as we did."

"It vas a huge discovery," Mrs. O said after swallowing the last drop of her coffee. "Ven dey opened up dah ground to build on to dah Louvre, dere vere dah roots of a castle. Towers and even a moat vere buried under it. And in dah moat, dey found a key. It looked like dah same key King Charles dah fifth's brother painted an image of in *Les Très Riches Heures,* but no von could find out vot it opened."

"Yes, here is a postcard of the painting I bought at the museum shop," said Madame Oursine, holding up a colorful oversized postcard. It showed a fairy-tale castle with some peasants working in the fields near it. Simone didn't see the key until Mrs. O pointed it out.

"Is in dis tower on dark moon side of castle."

There was a blue-gray moon on the horizon that was almost invisible, and next to Mrs. O's pink polished fingernail, one of the ten towers was topped with a gold spire that looked like a key. All ten towers had gold spires, but only one had such a unique shape. Simone took the necklace from inside her coat and held the key up to the painting. Identical.

Madame Oursine looked startled. "So there it is!" She held up another photograph. Someone had taken a photo of a key that looked like the one attached to Simone's prayer beads. "I wondered what happened to the other one," she said as Simone compared it with the picture.

"There was more than one?" Simone asked.

"Yes, more than one duplicate. Of course, they would never give us the one in the display case at the Louvre, so we had two duplicates created from this picture. I thought I'd have to disappoint you and say we didn't have another for you, because I didn't know you'd have this one."

"What do we need it for?" Simone asked.

"To follow your mother," Madame Oursine said and patted Simone's hand.

18

Labyrinth

W E CAN START with planning how to use your key, Simone," Madame Oursine said as she dangled the key on its rosary chain and watched it turn slowly. "I'll tell you what I know about what your mom had found out so far, and you can tell me any information or clues you have found. First, we both saw you through an open window in The Angel Line outside the Louvre. We thought something had gone wrong when you faded away and the window closed; we were very worried, but when we went inside and down into the old castle, we found something that gave a reason for it. The place where the window opened was directly above the spot in the castle moat where they found the key."

"The moat?"

"Yes, the one Mrs. O just mentioned. In the basement of the Louvre, there is the foundation of a tower with a moat around it. People who lived there long ago before the Louvre was built over it tossed in items they didn't want, or wanted to hide, and the museum has them all on display there. The curator told us they found the key hidden inside a bronze helmet. He said they believe a thief stole the helmet and later threw it into the moat for fear of being caught with it. He probably couldn't sell it or use it because the helmet belonged to King Charles the Sixth and had his special symbol engraved on it. Anyone who saw it would know it had been stolen from the king."

"What was the symbol?" Simone asked.

"A stag with wings."

"Wow! So do you think King Charles knew something about 'unusual' forms of transportation, like The Angel Lines?"

"Very possibly. I can't see any other reason for him to have hidden that key the way he did. Unfortunately, his key became lost and, in time, forgotten. But we found out what it opened because of your appearance. We had no idea there was an Angel Line that opened at the Louvre until we saw you, Simone."

Madame Oursine stood and opened a closet next to her chair. She took out a cloak similar to the nuns' habits the other ladies wore and wrapped it around herself. "Now we have matching disguises. Come. I'll show you what that key was made for."

They left the office and walked back down the silent hallway. Their four sets of footfalls made an unusually loud noise in the empty corridor. At the end of the hallway, Madame Oursine opened a large door. On the other side of the door was a beautiful spiral staircase made of marble steps and intricate brass railings. The walls were white and well lit by candle wall sconces and a grand chandelier overhead.

"This part of the building used to be the main ballroom. A cousin of King Charles the Sixth built it for parties and receptions away from the royal palace," said Madame Oursine.

"Can't you picture courtiers in their silk gowns and powdered wigs?" Madame Courbeau said gazing around at the gilded hall.

175
♪

Simone felt at home in the staircase at once, even though she had never lived in such a palace in her life. Maybe it was the golden glow that lit the room. It felt like any fresh summer morning in any house. Walking down the white steps, a lovely scent of bread baking in the oven wafted up from the kitchen where they had picked up their chocolate croissants. When she reached the bottom of the stairs she saw the second door from her dream.

The huge, dark red entrance door stood across a foyer with the gray flagstone floor partially covered with a green woven carpet. Next to the door, the vase of enormous pink tulips sat on a white marble-topped table. There under the table lay the sleepy brown hound dog that yawned and wagged its tail, but didn't bother to get up.

"Toc, you lazy watchdog," Madame Oursine chided.

"*Voilà!* There is your hound dog," whispered Madame Corbeau.

"Vot do vee do next?" asked Mrs. O.

"We open it," Simone said breathlessly.

"Be my guest," Madame Oursine said, motioning Simone forward.

She stepped up to the door. As in her dream, the brass doorknob turned easily, but the deadbolt lock was sticky. She finally opened it and then shoved her shoulder against the heavy door.

Stepping outside, Simone saw they were in a walled-off section of courtyard, separated from the one they had entered earlier. As in her dream, trees and flowers bloomed beside a stone path that led to a circular walkway in the center of the courtyard. But there was no entrance to a great cathedral here as there had been in her dream.

"Do you know vot that path is?" asked Mrs. O.

"I've seen it in my dream, but I've also heard something about them. What are they called?"

Mrs. O answered, "It is called a prayer labyrinth. You pray as you valk dah circles and dah circles inside dah circles."

Madame Corbeau pointed to the circles of the path, tracing their looping pattern in the air and added, "Walking through it by following its path is like going on a pilgrimage—an inner pilgrimage to the center of our being. At the center of this one is a rosette design, like the rose windows we saw at Notre-Dame. They are symbols of many things, including the revealing of secrets.

"We use a prayer labyrinth as a way to meditate, pray, and think through our decisions. You have to walk around the turning path through all four sections several times before reaching the center. It symbolizes the world and all its twists and turns, the troubles and mysteries we go through on our walk through this life. When you enter the labyrinth, it is like being born. When you reach the center, it is as if you've reached Heaven."

Madame Oursine added an even more interesting reason to explore the circles laid out by the stone path. "We believe the real path that leads us through life is God's grace—a path chosen for us by our Maker. So the labyrinth is also a symbol of grace. But this particular path has more to it than just symbols—at its center, hidden in the stones, is a lock that fits your key."

"What are we waiting for? Let's go see what it unlocks. It must have something to do with my mom's disappearance." Simone pulled the key and necklace from under her coat, ready to go.

"Just a moment," Madame Corbeau said, putting her hand over Simone's, covering the key. "I think we need to hear the rest of the story. There is more, yes?"

Madame Oursine frowned and leaned toward them. She whispered, "This prayer path is very old; so old that it may have been laid at the time Paris was founded, or at

177
♪

least during the time of King Charles' great-grandfather, Charlemagne. After we found the key at the Louvre castle ruins, we studied the helmet in which it was hidden.

"In its pattern we found a mathematical formula based on a series of four numbers, like the four sections of the labyrinth. After studying that formula, we believed that the secret to opening The Angel Line was to walk through each of the four sections and touch the key on every fourth stone as if bowing in prayer. We believed this path would open a door in The Angel Lines that would let Heaven's answers to many prayers through, not only the ones our company has been praying for France, but for places around the world."

"No, no, that's not right," said Simone. Her "truth sensor" told her there was something wrong in the explanation—there was something missing in what Madame Oursine was saying, like a missing puzzle piece. "What I saw in my dream was four people walking the labyrinth. I don't think the secret to the labyrinth has as much to do with numbers of things as with numbers of people." As soon as she said it, Simone could feel the truth of her interpretation ringing her truth sensor like a chime.

"So dere vas a problem ven Mandy used her key alone?" Mrs. O asked.

"Yes. Oh, dear. We were wrong about the formula, obviously," Madame Oursine said, her eyes filling up with tears. "I was so proud of our detective work—Mandy warned me it felt wrong to her, to her sense of what is true. And she was right. As soon as she put the key into the lock, she disappeared. Right there in the center of the labyrinth.

"I called out to her, and ran across the labyrinth to try to stop her or follow her, but I was too late. She faded into a mist and I was left standing there alone. I haven't seen her since, though I have walked the path and prayed to follow her or bring her back. She listened to me instead of her inner voice—her gift. It was my fault."

Mrs. O put her arm around Simone's shoulders. "So ve are vorried about vot vill happen if you use your key."

"I'm worried, too," Simone admitted. "But I have to take the risk to try to help Mom. I'm sure that's why I was sent or called here."

Madame Corbeau agreed. "We think so, too, dear. And we believe we were called to help you. I think we were the women you saw in your dream dressed as nuns. We want to protect you and go with you to your mother if possible."

"Vee vill lead the vay," Mrs. O said. "You follow us and vee pray the prayer you heard in your dream—it vas the prayer of St. Patrick. Christ vill go before us and behind us."

Madame Oursine nodded her head and frowned gravely. "The only questions that remain are where we will go and what we will do when we get there."

Madame Corbeau touched her on the shoulder as if to comfort the worried younger woman. "I think we can tell something about that from Simone's dream. After she followed the women dressed as nuns through the prayer labyrinth, she found herself in front of a cathedral door, and inside that door was an altar with a rose window behind it. Simone, think about that scene. There is no cathedral door here in this little courtyard, so we must assume that The Angel Line that starts in the middle of this labyrinth ends in front of the one you saw in your dream."

Simone had not put the last pieces of her dream together until that very minute. Maybe it had taken that long to remember enough detail to do so, but she was suddenly very sure she had seen that immense door in both her dreaming and waking worlds.

"It was Notre-Dame Cathedral!" she shouted. "I must have been standing right on Point Zero in my dream. I didn't remember it at all when we were there, but now I do. Maybe I had to see this place to remember that one."

"So, King Charles had a secret vay to get to church?" asked Mrs. O.

"That makes sense," said Madame Oursine. "King Charles and his family must have built the labyrinth to mark the spot that would take them back and forth from his secret prayer garden to the place they went for spiritual guidance, to Notre-Dame, where his confessor and priest could help them or hide them from trouble. There was so much violence here in the name of religion over hundreds of years—Catholics against Protestants, atheists against Catholics, revolutionaries against the monarchy, and then Germans against Jews and the Resistance. Even at the beginning of everything there were tribes like the Celts, who were crushed by the Roman invaders. That's one reason there are so many secret passages and hiding places in old castles throughout the land."

Madame Corbeau patted Simone's hand. "So now that we know where this escape Line goes and how to use it, we shouldn't waste any more time. Simone, you follow us as we say St. Patrick's famous prayer, then put your key into the lock at the center of the labyrinth. According to your dream, we will all end up at the Cathedral together."

181
♪

19

Secret Angel

THE THREE WOMEN bowed their heads and led the way around the four loops of the path praying:

"Christ be with me:
Christ within me,
Christ behind me,
Christ before me,
Christ beside me,
Christ to win me,
Christ to comfort and restore me,
Christ beneath me,
Christ above me,
Christ in quiet,
Christ in danger,

Christ in hearts of all that love me,
Christ in mouth of friend and stranger."

Simone followed them, repeating the same words over and over with them until they all stood at the center of the pattern. Madame Corbeau pointed to a small slot in the rock that marked the center of the rose pattern. "Now, Simone."

Simone's hand was shaking a little as she knelt on one knee and slid the key into the rock's keyhole. She tried to turn it as she would a door lock, but found it wasn't necessary. As soon as she heard the sound of the metal key scraping into the slot, everything around her started to fade, just as it had at the golf course in Ohio. Everything dissolved into fog except for the three ladies next to her, the key, and the paving stones of the prayer labyrinth, which became more colorful and glowed at the edges. The labyrinth seemed to grow larger and spread out like ripples from the center, where Simone held the key in the lock.

She gripped the key's handle tightly to balance herself as the scene around her made its dizzying transformation. Instead of feeling as if she were moving to another point through The Lines, it felt as if the world were moving while she remained in place. The three ladies in black seemed to sway with the changing scene and Simone realized their clothing was moving because of a mild breeze.

The sheltering wall of the garden disappeared, and in its place appeared a wide plaza with paving stones

183
♪

glowing in the pattern of the labyrinth. Facing the place where Simone knelt were the immense wooden doors of Notre-Dame Cathedral, and the place where her key was enclosed by the lock now had an inscription that read: *Point Zero.*

"Dere vas a hidden prayer labyrinth at Point Zero!" Mrs. O whispered. People around the plaza were going about their business as if they had not noticed the "nuns" and Simone at all. Simone pulled the key from the lock and stood up. The patterned stones began to fade back into their normal steel gray color and no one milling around the place seemed to have noticed their unusual glow.

Madame Corbeau motioned to Simone and the others to follow her. "Come. Let's take the steps your dream showed you—before anyone has a chance to stop us."

Simone followed the women around the circle and out the other side of the fading prayer path pattern. The path continued to the third door of her familiar dream. This door stood open and led into the magnificent Notre-Dame Cathedral, its far wall nearly filled by a huge, shining rose window made of stained glass in every the color of the rainbow. As her companions in black walked through the door, they disappeared into the dark interior, as if becoming part of the shadows on either side of the window, the great room's main source of light.

Dozens of little, white candle jars glowed on long tables beside the door. As Simone entered, she automatically did the things she had done many times in her dream, as if she were dreaming now. She picked up one of the candles and carried it so she could more clearly see the aisle before her. She held the small light carefully in one hand and her saxophone case in the other, as she walked toward the altar under the rose window. When she reached it, she stood still for a minute looking up at the enchanting glass design.

Then she remembered what to do next, because she heard the music. It was her cue. That soft, pure melody, so lovely it brought tears to her eyes, drifted out over the altar and seemed to wrap its message around her heart. At first she thought it was a saxophone, but the tone was different from any instrument she'd ever heard. She could not imagine what combination of instruments would be capable of producing such a sound. The melody was more intricate and, at the same time simpler, than earthly music. Yet there was something missing—the music sounded to Simone like a question waiting to be answered.

185
♪

Then the playing stopped, but the music remained— in Simone's soul, as if it had lit a candle that still burned there, like the one she carried with her from the door-way. It was as if the music was waiting for her reply. She looked around trying to remember her dream and where the music had been coming from—that was when she noticed a door behind the altar on the right side.

A ribbon of light was coming from under the door and she could see a flicker of movement. Someone was standing behind it—the fourth door of her dream. She knew that, to find her mom, she had to hear it again and see the musician who created it. As she watched, the ribbon of light began to grow larger. The door was opening.

The light from the little room was so bright in the dim sanctuary that Simone could not see the face of the person standing inside. She could see only the figure's outline. It stepped out of the brightness into the room and looked around as if blinded. Then Simone could see clearly who the person was.

"Mom!" Simone called out.

She ran to her mom and grabbed her in the best hug ever. "Simone? What are you doing here? And where is here?" Mom said in a weak voice.

"Don't you know?"

Her mom shook her head and looked around, as if trying to get her bearings as her eyes adjusted to the dim light. "Last I remember, I was at the youth hostel . . . with this key. I was counting fours, and fours within fours. I couldn't stop. It seemed to go on forever." She held up a key that matched Simone's key. "Then I heard you calling me and the fours just crumbled away. That was weird, so strange. I thought I had the clues all figured out, but the solution wouldn't present itself and it wouldn't let me go."

Unlike Simone's dream, the ladies dressed in nuns' clothing did not stay in the shadows. As soon as they realized Simone's mom had come out of the room, the women ran to her side. Madame Oursine was the first to reach them and hugged Mom, crying and laughing. "Oh, Mandy, you are back. I was so worried."

"You must have been caught inside The Lines," Madame Corbeau said. "It wasn't an enemy spy we needed to fear. What caused the problem was a false clue . . ."

"A false clue and false confidence in our own sleuthing. We had the wrong formula, Mandy," said Madame Oursine. "I'm sorry. I was so sure of myself. I should have listened to you when you said it felt wrong."

"But how did you find me?" Mom asked.

"It was Simone's dream," Madame Oursine said.

"But how did you know about the dream before I came?" Simone asked. "Mom, how did you know what to write in the note you left me?"

"That's easy," her mom replied. "I had a dream of my own when I was staying at Madame Corbeau's apartment. I saw you telling her about a dream you had, and then she said it would help you find me."

"And it did," Simone said, hugging her mom again. "That reminds me, did you see anyone else in that room? An angel, perhaps?"

Mom shook her head. "Just fours repeating themselves into infinity . . . but I see someone now." She pointed over Simone's shoulder toward the alcove, where another figure was coming out of the dazzling light into the main cathedral.

The being held an instrument that glowed golden as flames of fire. It was the angel of Simone's dream: wings, glowing robe, halo, and all. It held the strange musical instrument that looked like it had been carved from a ram's horn. But this time he or she did not lightly give

187
♪

the instrument to Simone. The angel spoke a challenge, or maybe an invitation: "What do you have in your hand?"

"You mean my instrument case? My saxophone?" Simone asked.

The creature did something that looked like a wink—but Simone couldn't believe an angel would wink. It definitely nodded, though, and the challenge was clear. She knew he or she wanted her to play. And she wanted to play, to remember the music of her dream. As she opened her case and put the sax together, the angel began the beautiful melody Simone had heard earlier. The question it posed was still haunting her. *Will you say the things your heart believes? Will you put them into music and make them real?* Suddenly, Simone knew that doing so would cast aside all her doubt about God and her family and her life.

That was it. The missing part of the melody.

Simone lifted her instrument and, as soon as she began to play, she knew how to say what needed to be said. It was a melody she had heard in her dreams, and now she realized it was her own spirit singing. She added it as subtle as a spring breeze, and it had the same effect on the music as warm breath on ice.

The whole composition began to melt into fluidity like a frozen brook coming back to life after winter. Everything she'd played in the past year, with Adam and all her friends, with people she barely knew, such as Mr. Cantor and Firebelly Floyd, began to speak through the

188
♪

music that came pouring out of the two instruments. She told about them in her notes and the angel echoed what Simone knew and added more—it sounded like what God knew about each of them as individuals and together. It told about Simone and how she was because of those people, the changes meeting and parting with people had made in her life. How she'd grown because of each new experience and what she'd found through each person, their own special treasure adding to the richness of the song as a whole.

Then the melody grew until it told about people she didn't know and how the circles of the lives that had touched hers connected to theirs. The story seemed to wrap itself around the world, circle by circle, like The Lines. She could picture the music flowing out over the whole earth in circles that expanded like ripples. As The Lines on Earth became filled with music, they seemed to burst upward, to the stars and on to the heavens. Then, suddenly, there were answering notes descending from above. An infinite number of voices began to join the song and Simone remembered the Scripture passage about the Christmas shepherds that says, "A host of heavenly angels joined in and sang, 'Glory to God on high, blessed is he who comes in the name of the Lord.'" They seemed to lift the melody and carry it off with them until Simone knew her part in the piece was finished.

"Do not be afraid," the angel said. "They bring tidings of great joy. The good news that was born into the earth two thousand years ago is still being told. It is still

189
♪

growing in the hearts of men and angels until all is sung, until all is said. It will open doors no man can close, and its great love and power will open hearts no man can unlock. You are part of the song and the song is part of you, as it is with me and all who serve God and give their lives to him. You will see many souls set free because you obeyed. Many will be set free whom you will not see with your eyes, but will know with your spirit. This is a great mystery and you have played your part well."

For the first time, Simone felt absolutely satisfied with the music she had played—no regrets, no further revisions needed, no rushing off to the practice room to correct her imperfections. It was as if the music had spoken through her, asked the questions it needed to ask, and had answered itself completely. There was no need to say more.

190

The angel bent down and held out the ram's horn, offering her the beautiful instrument. She had a sudden inspiration and offered the angel her beloved saxophone in return, looking over her shoulder at her mom, who was smiling in approval. The angel did not exactly smile, but just began to glow until so bright Simone could barely see. As she lifted the saxophone, the angel held out the ram's horn and the two instruments met. The horn seemed to melt into her saxophone, the two becoming one instrument. As they did, the angel disappeared into the bright light.

Simone looked at her saxophone. It looked just as it had before, as it had always looked, but it felt different.

Like her. She saw her own reflection in it and thought how strange it was that she looked the same, even though she had been born into something entirely new and something entirely new had been born in her that night.

"That instrument was made for you, Simone," her mom's reflection smiled in the old sax as she laid her hands on her daughter's shoulders. They hugged and laughed.

"Ah, laughter is the music of angels," Madame Corbeau's voice floated out of the darkness, and she followed it into the candlelight with Mrs. O right behind her. As her friends appeared, Simone saw a familiar shimmering at the edge of the darkness.

Mrs. O saw it, too. "Vell, vell, time to go," she said pointing to a silver path opening right down the aisle of the church. She and Madame took off their nuns' habits, revealing their ordinary dresses underneath and hung them neatly on a prayer rail. "Coming, ladies?" Mrs. O asked, tossing a handful of crumbs from her apron pockets and stepping out onto the path of tiny fish.

"I'm ready," Simone said cheerfully. She took her mom's hand and they walked the path together behind Mrs. O and Madame Corbeau. They waved goodbye to Madame Oursine, who watched them go, growing smaller and smaller as they walked away. Mom looked amazed, and Simone had plenty of time to tell her all about how they arrived and many other things about her adventures as they walked home. By the time they saw the wall of the band room and rows of lockers ahead,

191
♪

Mom was all caught up on the events that led up to Simone's arrival in Paris. The silver path slowly faded and they found themselves standing on solid floor.

"Home!" Simone and Mom cried out together. Then they heard a commotion from the hallway and the big doors to the band room burst open. Adam, Moby, Greg, and Conan stomped through yelling Simone's name.

"Hey, your mom's back," Adam said as he saw the ladies. "Did you make it in time to hear Simone play?"

"Uh, yes. I did hear her play," Mom said, nudging Simone.

"It was great," Adam said and gave Simone a big hug. "And we told Wembly we are not interested in playing pop music for some other contest he's organizing, even though he swore we'd 'never be able to buy publicity like that' anywhere else."

"We have a good sound of our own and we don't need to change it for marketing purposes," Greg said. "Let's just keep at it together and see where it takes us."

Moby nodded, then suggested, "I think it's time for some real Blueberry Koffee at the shop. Who's coming with me?"

Everyone accepted his invitation except Mom. They dropped her off at the house, where she found her husband sitting on the couch grading papers with every light in the house turned on.

Look for Book One in the Angel Light™ series of novels by Pat Matuszak

Angela Clarkson has always been intrigued by mysteries, but lately her life has turned into one mystery after another. Her friends in the horse club are giving up riding horses, and this bothers her. Angela's family doesn't seem to speak her language anymore, or maybe it's that she suddenly doesn't understand theirs. Then a mysterious stranger gains a powerful influence over her best friend; this stranger turns out to be at the center of a secret involving her little town—one that concerns the line drawn between heaven and hell. Angela and her friends are caught in the middle of a conflict between spiritual beings who are keepers of that secret. Her greatest mystery is solved when she learns the difference between an angel of light and an angel of lies.

www.livinginkbooks.com